"I'd like us to be friends."

His hand rested on the table, so close to hers.

She stared at his long fingers. She'd always loved his hands. They showed strength. Seeing them made her wonder what they would feel like on her.

She pushed the thought away. "No."

"Abby, come on."

"I have that level of trust and understanding with Derrick because there is nothing else in the way. Nothing else between us because I don't have any other feelings for him." The words echoed in her head. She closed her eyes for a second before opening them again, hoping she'd only thought them. But no, there he was. Staring at her. Clear that he heard every syllable.

His eyebrow lifted. "But you do feel something for me?"

The look on his face. Was that satisfaction or hope? She couldn't tell. Didn't want to know. She never meant to open that door. Thinking it and saying it were two very different things, and she'd blown it. Now she rushed to try to fix the damage. "Did. That's over."

"Is it?"

* * *

Reunion with Benefits is part of
The Jameson Heirs trilogy
from HelenKay Dimon!

Dear Reader,

It's time to return to Washington, DC, and the lives of the wealthy, powerful and very dysfunctional Jameson family.

The brothers are trying to wrestle the family business away from their troublemaking and mostly absent father. He's busy making demands and protecting secrets he's not ready to tell. Each brother has a task he needs to complete, but their father's lies and games make that tough.

Now it's Spencer's turn. He's back in town and ready to do whatever needs to be done to help his brothers. That means seeing Abby—the woman he can't forget. Rumors, anger and old wounds haunt Abby and Spence. He wants to sweet-talk her and move forward, but she is not buying it. Abby is strong and smart...and really ticked off. She is just fine with them remaining enemies and never talking again, which means Spence has a lot of work to do to win her back and work his way through the mess his father created. You almost have to feel bad for Spence...almost.

I hope you enjoy Spence and Abby's enemies-to-lovers story.

Happy reading!

HelenKay

HELENKAY DIMON

—

REUNION WITH BENEFITS

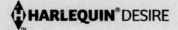

**Recycling programs
for this product may
not exist in your area.**

ISBN-13: 978-1-335-97157-9

Reunion with Benefits

Copyright © 2018 by HelenKay Dimon

This edition published by arrangement with Harlequin Books S.A.

For questions and comments about the quality of this book, please contact us at CustomerService@Harlequin.com.

Printed in U.S.A.

HARLEQUIN®
www.Harlequin.com

HelenKay Dimon is a divorce lawyer turned full-time author. Her bestselling and award-winning books have been showcased in numerous venues, including the *Washington Post* and *Cosmopolitan*. She is an RT Reviewers' Choice Best Book Award winner and has been a finalist for the Romance Writers of America's RITA® Award multiple times.

Books by HelenKay Dimon

Harlequin Desire

The Jameson Heirs

Pregnant by the CEO
Reunion with Benefits

Harlequin Intrigue

Corcoran Team

Fearless
Ruthless
Relentless
Lawless
Traceless

Visit her Author Profile page at Harlequin.com, or helenkaydimon.com, for more titles.

One

Spencer Jameson wasn't accustomed to being ignored.

He'd been back in Washington, DC, for three weeks. The plan was to buzz into town for just enough time to help out his oldest brother, Derrick, and then leave again.

That's what Spence did. He moved on. Too many days back in the office meant he might run into his father. Eldrick Jameson was the family patriarch, a recently retired businessman on his fourth wife... and the main reason Spence wanted to be anywhere but the DC metro area most of the time.

But dear old Dad was not the problem this trip. The new wife had convinced him to move to Tortola, an island over fifteen hundred miles away. That was almost enough distance, though Spence would have been fine with more.

No, Spence had a different target in mind today. Abigail Rowe, the woman currently pretending he didn't exist.

He used the keys he borrowed from the office manager to open the door to the abandoned elementary school in northeast DC. The building had been empty for two years, caught in a ball of red tape over government regulations and environmental concerns. Derrick wanted the company to buy it and do a complete internal rebuild to turn the massive property into something usable. Spence was on-site meeting the head of the team assigned to make it happen… the head being *her*, and she actually didn't know he was attending.

He followed the sound of voices, a man's deep laughter and the steady rumble of a lighter female one. Careful not to give away his presence, Spence leaned against the outer hall wall and peeked into what he guessed used to be the student dining hall. Paint peeled off the stucco walls. Old posters were half ripped down and half hanging by old tape. Rows of luncheon tables and benches had been replaced with one folding table and a couple of chairs that didn't look sturdy enough to hold an adult.

A woman stood there—*the* woman. She wore a sleek navy suit with a skirt that stopped just above the knee. She embodied the perfect mix of professionalism and sexiness. The flash of bare long legs brought back memories. He could see her only from behind right now but that angle looked really good to him.

Just as he remembered.

Her brown hair reached past her shoulders and ended in a gentle curl. Where it used to be darker, it now had light brown highlights. Strands shifted over her shoulder as she bent down to show the man standing next to her—almost on top of her—something in a file.

Not that the other man was paying attention to whatever she said. His gaze traveled over her. As she talked and pointed, he leaned back slightly and stared at her legs then up higher.

Spence couldn't exactly blame him, but nothing about that look was professional or appropriate. The lack of respect was not okay. The guy's joking charm gave way to something much more territorial and heated. As far as Spence was concerned, the other man was begging for a punch in the face.

As if he sensed his behavior was under a microscope, the man glanced up and turned. Spence got a full-on view of him. He looked like every blond-haired, blue-eyed guy in his midthirties who hung out in bars around the city looking for young Capitol Hill interns to date. Good-looking in a still-brags-about-his-college-days kind of way. That sort of thing was big in this town, as if where you went to school defined you a decade or so later.

Point was, Spence knew the type. Charming, resourceful and looking for an easy lay. He knew because he'd been that guy. He just grew out of it well before he hit thirty.

The other man's eyebrows rose and he hesitated for a second before hitting Spence with a big flashy smile. "Good afternoon."

At the intrusion, Abby spun around. Her expression switched from surprised to flat-mouthed anger in the span of two seconds. "Spencer."

It was not exactly a loving welcome, but for a second he couldn't breathe. The air stammered in his lungs. Seeing her now hit him like a body blow. He had to fight off the urge to rub a hand over his stomach.

They'd worked together for months, every day with him wanting to break the office conduct rules and ask her out. He got close but backed off, sensing he was crossing a line. Then she made a move. A stolen touch here. A kiss there. He'd battled with his control and waited because he needed to be careful. But he'd wanted her from the first moment he saw her. Now, months later, the attraction still lingered... which ticked him off.

Her ultimate betrayal hadn't killed his interest in her, no matter how much he wanted it to.

"Spencer Jameson?" The guy walked toward Spence with his arm extended. "Excellent to meet you."

"Is it?" Spencer shook the guy's hand as he stared at Abby. He wasn't sure what was going on. Abby was supposed to be here with her team. Working. This felt like something else.

"I didn't realize you'd be joining us." Her deep voice stayed even, almost monotone.

If she was happy to see him, she sure hid it well. Frustration pounded off her and filled the room. The tension ratcheted up to a suffocating degree even though none of them moved.

Spence tried not to let his gaze linger on her. Tried not to show how seeing her again affected him. "Where are the others?"

The man did a quick look around the empty room. "Excuse me?"

"Derrick told me—"

"Rylan Stamford is the environmental engineer who is performing the site assessment." She even managed to make that sentence sound angry and clipped.

The job title didn't really explain why Rylan looked ready to jump on Abby a second ago. Spence sensed Rylan's mind wasn't only on the job. "Our assessment?"

"The city's," Abby said. "Rylan isn't employed by us."

Rylan's smile grew wider. "But I've been working very closely with Abby."

Yeah, Spence kind of hated this guy. "I'm sure."

Abby exhaled loud enough to bring the conversation to a halt. She turned back to the table and started piling the paperwork in a neat stack. "Did you need something, Spence?"

She clearly wanted to be in control of the conversation and them seeing each other again. Unfortunately for her, so did he. And that started now. "We have a meeting."

She slowly turned around again. "We do?"

"Just the two of us." The idea was risky and maybe a little stupid, but he needed to stay in town until his soon-to-be sister-in-law gave birth. Derrick's fiancée's pregnancy was high-risk and Spence promised to help, to take some of the pressure off Derrick.

"Oh, I see."

That tone... Abby may as well have threatened to hit him with her car. She definitely was not happy to see him. Spence got that. "No, you don't."

She sighed. "Oh, really?"

If words had the force of a knife, he'd be sliced to pieces. She'd treated him to a prickly, unwelcome greeting and, if anything, the coolness had turned even icier since then.

The reaction struck him as interesting, infuriating even, since *he* was the injured party here. She cheated on him. Well, not technically, since they weren't officially going out back then, but she'd done the one thing he could not stand—she used him to climb the ladder to get to a stronger, more powerful Jameson: his father.

Spence glanced at Rylan. He stood there in his perfectly pressed gray suit and purple tie. He had the right watch. The right haircut. He'd shined his shoes and combed his hair. Nothing—not one damn thing—was out of place on this guy.

Clearly Rylan hoped this was a date or the prelude to a date and not an informal afternoon business meeting.

Well, that was enough of that.

"Are you done here?" Spence asked Rylan, making sure his tone suggested the answer should be yes.

"Absolutely." Rylan's sunny disposition didn't dim one bit. He put a hand on Abby's arm and gave it a squeeze. "I'll call you tomorrow so we can go over the list of concerns." His hand dropped as he faced Spence again and nodded. "Mr. Jameson."

Yeah, whatever. "Rylan."

Spence watched the engineer leave. He'd never had such a sudden negative reaction to a person in his life. Rylan could have said anything and Spence would have disliked him.

Abby leaned back with her hands resting on the table on either side of her hips. "Heavy-handed as always, I see."

Facing her head-on, without a buffer, tested the defenses he'd thrown up against her. He shouldn't care. It shouldn't mean anything. If only his brain and his body would listen to that order.

Despite standing ten feet apart, Spence felt a familiar sensation spark inside him. Desire mixed with lust and a bit of confusion. The intensity hit him full force.

"Did I interrupt your date?"

She rolled her eyes. "Right. Because I'm incapable of meeting with a man without crawling all over him."

"You said it, not me."

She exhaled loud enough to let him know she had better things to do. "What do you want?"

She didn't back down. He'd always loved that about her. The boss-employee boundaries didn't mean much to her. If she had a thought, she said it. If she disagreed, she let him know. She'd been tactful in not making angry announcements in the office lunchroom, but she wasn't the type to coddle a man's ego, either.

He'd found that sexy. So sexy even as his life crumbled around him and his relationship with his father, which had never been good, disintegrated.

"Is that how you talk to your boss?" He figured he may as well try to reestablish the lines between them. Like it or not, they had to figure out a way to tolerate each other.

For him, it meant ignoring the way she walked and the sound of her voice. Forgetting that he once was willing to go against his father to be with her. But he had to smash all of those feelings, all that vulnerability, now.

"Is that what you are? Last I checked, you ran out of the office and never looked back. If this were a cartoon, you would have left a man-size hole in the wall." She smiled for the first time.

"I'd had a surprise." As if that was the right word for seeing the woman you wanted locked in the arms of a father who turned out to be a constant disappointment.

She pushed away from the table. Without looking at him, she finished straightening the stacks of files.

Made each edge line up. "You still think you're the victim then?"

"You were kissing my father."

She glanced over at him again. "Why are you here, Spence?"

No denial, but just like the last time they'd talked—yelled and argued with each other—and a hint of sadness settled in her big brown eyes. Her shoulders fell a bit and for just a second, she didn't look like the confident, in-charge woman he knew her to be.

He had no idea what that meant. But he did have a job to do. "This is an important project and—"

"I mean in DC." She picked up the stack of files and hugged them tight to her chest. "Are you back permanently?"

He hated that question. Derrick had asked it. People at the company had asked. The guy at the rental car company wanted to know. Spence gave her the same answer he'd given to everyone for three weeks. "Derrick needs some help."

"Huh." She frowned at him as her gaze wandered over his face. "I don't really think of you as the type to drop everything and come running to assist someone else."

Charming. "It's not as if we know each other all that well, do we?"

"I guess not." She bent down and picked up her bag. She looked cleaned up and ready to bolt.

"Derrick's fiancée has a health issue," he said.

The anger drained from Abby's face. So did some

of the color. She took a step forward with her hand out, but dropped her arm right before she touched him. "Did something new go wrong with the pregnancy?"

"You know about that?" Sure, the pregnancy had been on the gossip sites. One of the playboy Jameson heirs settling down was big news. Their lives had been followed and dissected for years. Every mistake highlighted. Every girlfriend photographed. The rumors, the lies. But the family hadn't confirmed the pregnancy because it was too soon and too personal. "Are you two friends?"

Abby's expression went blank. "You sound horrified by the idea."

Admittedly, he was acting like a jerk, as if everything was about him. Ellie, Derrick's fiancée, needed support. Spence got that. But still... "Well, it will be a bit uncomfortable, don't you think?"

"As uncomfortable as this conversation?"

For some reason, the response knocked the wind right out of him. He almost smiled, but managed to beat it back at the last minute. "Look, we're going to need to get along."

She shrugged. "Why?"

Man, she had not changed one bit. *"Why?"*

"You've been back for three weeks and we've successfully avoided each other. I say we keep doing that."

She sounded aloof and unaffected, but he could see her white-knuckle grip on the files. Much tighter and she'd cut off circulation to her fingers. In fact, this close he saw everything. The flecks of gold around the outside of her eyes. The slight tremor in her hands.

He could smell her, that heady mix of ginger and something sweet. It was her shampoo and it floated to him now.

He inhaled, trying to calm the heartbeat pounding in his ears. "Now who's running?"

"Do you really want to have this conversation? Because we can." She took one more step. The move left little more than a whisper of air between them. "I'm not the one who saw something, misinterpreted it and then threw the mother of all hissy fits."

The air in the room closed in around him. He could actually feel it press against his back. "Misinterpreted?"

"You're offended by my word choice?"

"You were kissing my father!" He shouted the accusation loud enough to make the walls shake.

A sharp silence descended on them right after. In the quiet, she retreated both physically and emotionally. The air seemed to seep right out of her.

"That's what you think you saw." Not a question. Not really even a statement. She said the words and let them sit there.

The adrenaline shooting through him refused to ease off. "Hell, yes!"

"You can let yourself out." She walked around him and headed for the door.

"Hey." His hand brushed against her arm. He dropped it again when she glared at him. "Fine. No touching."

"None." Which sounded like *not ever*.

Regret plowed into him. He came here for them to talk this out. He'd gone into the computer and looked up her schedule. Came here unannounced, thinking he'd have the upper hand.

"I want us to be civil toward each other," he said as he struggled to bring his voice back under control.

She shook her head. "No."

"What?" He'd been the one to offer the olive branch. He hadn't insisted on an apology or that she take responsibility. But she still came out swinging and didn't stop.

"You lied to me," she said in a voice growing stronger with each word.

For a second, his brain misfired. He couldn't think of a response. "When?"

"You let me believe you weren't *that guy*, but you are. Rich, entitled, ready to bolt, tied to his daddy and desperate for approval." She counted out his perceived sins on her fingers.

That fast his temper skyrocketed again. Heat flushed through him "That's enough."

"The suggestion still stands. We ignore each other."

"Does that mean you're going to leave every room I enter? Get off projects I'm overseeing?"

She shrugged. "That all works for me."

No, he was not going to be pushed into a corner. He was the boss. He wasn't the one who screwed everything up.

He pointed at her. "You did this to us."

Her mouth dropped open. For a second, she didn't

say anything, and then she clenched her teeth to-gether. "You're unbelievable."

She slipped by him a second time. Got the whole way to the doorway.

"Stop trying to storm off, and talk to me." He didn't try to grab her but he did want to.

She was absolutely infuriating. Every word she said pushed him until the frustration mixed with the attraction and it all pounded in his head.

"Okay." She whipped around and faced him again. "You want me to talk, try this. You're no better than your father."

The words sliced through him. Ripped right through the layers of clothing and skin.

"I guess you should be the one to compare us since you kissed both of us." When she just stood there, staring at him, he wanted to lash out even harder. "What, no comeback?"

"Stay out of my way."

"Or?"

"Don't push me, Spence. Other people might be afraid of you or want to impress you, but I know better." She shook her head. "What you need is for someone to kick your butt. Keep talking and I will."

Two

Everything was weird now. For the last few weeks, Abby didn't think twice about heading over to Ellie's house on the tree-lined street in Georgetown for a visit. She lived with and was engaged to Derrick Jameson and their high-risk pregnancy had people at work, their friends—everyone—on edge.

Derrick was Spence's older brother, and Spence was the nightmare that just wouldn't go away, so Abby was torn. Being friends with someone tied that closely to the man who broke her heart promised more pain. That was the last thing Abby needed.

Ellie and Abby met by accident, really. Someone wrongly suggested Abby and Derrick were having a "thing" and Ellie stopped by Abby's office to apologize for getting her dragged into their personal business and someone else's vendetta. Abby still didn't understand what happened, but she was grateful for the warning and the show of trust from Ellie, a woman who didn't know her at all at that point. That was three weeks ago and they'd been friends since.

Trust was more than she ever got from Spence, the man she'd planned to date, sleep with, before he stormed off refusing to listen to her months ago. The awful day played out so clearly on a loop in her head.

Panic and frustration whirled together in her mind. "It's not what you think."

"I have eyes, Abby." And that furious gaze switched back and forth between her and his father... and his hand on her waist. The noise rumbling out of Spence almost sounded like a snarl. "You want the top of the Jameson food chain? He's all yours. Good luck."

She tried to follow him but Eldrick held on. "Spence, wait—"

"I told you." Eldrick smiled down at her as she yanked her arm out of his grip. "You're going after the wrong Jameson."

"I'm so happy you came..." Ellie's smile fell as she talked. "What happened?"

The memory blinked out at the sound of Ellie's voice. Abby snapped back into reality as she stood in the doorway to Ellie and Derrick's bedroom, holding a box of brownies from that place in Foggy Bottom that Ellie had raved about a few days before.

Abby had no idea what conversation she missed as her mind wandered, but both Derrick and Ellie stared at her. Ellie was cuddled up in a blanket in the center of the gigantic never-seen-a-king-size-bed-that-big bed with pillows tucked around her body and the television remote control in her hand. Derrick, still wearing his dress pants and button-down shirt, sat next to her. Not on top of her, but close enough for the intimacy, the closeness, to flow around them. His only nod to being home and not at work came in the removal of his tie. It lay over the armrest of the overstuffed chair by the bed.

"Nothing." That seemed like a reasonable response to most things, so Abby went with that as her answer.

"Huh." Ellie made a face. "You look furious."

Derrick let out a long breath. "So, Spence."

"Definitely Spence," Ellie said with a nod.

Well, they weren't wrong. Derrick and Spence were brothers and her bosses. But still. "I don't know how you two are related."

"We're actually a lot alike." Derrick smiled at first but when Abby stood there, not moving, Derrick bit his bottom lip. "But I can see that's the wrong answer."

"Did something happen?" Ellie patted an empty space on the bed, inviting Abby farther into the room to take a seat.

Seeing the two of them, with Derrick's arm resting on the pillows behind Ellie and his fingers slipping into her hair and massaging her neck, struck Abby with the force of a slap. A pang of something... jealousy, regret, longing...moved through her. She couldn't identify the feeling or grab on to it long enough to assess it. But the idea that she was interrupting did crash on top of her.

She was about to drop the brownies and run when she saw both of their faces. The concern. Derrick was the big boss and he deserved to know Spence hadn't really done anything wrong. This time.

She shook her head. "Nothing, really. He walked onto my job site unannounced."

Derrick winced. "Yeah, about that."

Ellie's head slowly turned and she pinned Derrick with a you're-in-trouble glare. "What did you do?"

"With you being on bed rest—"

"Don't blame me," Ellie warned.

"Let me try again." Derrick, the tough, no-nonsense boss who sent employees scurrying, cleared his throat. "Since I can't be in the office as much as usual right now—"

Ellie's sigh echoed around the room. "You're still blaming me."

They were so cute, so perfectly in sync, that Abby took pity on Derrick. "Let me guess. Spence is overseeing some of the projects now that he's back in town."

Derrick closed his eyes for a second before opening them again. Relief poured off him. "Thank you and yes."

She wasn't willing to let him *all* the way off the hook. "Like the one I'm in charge of."

"The key phrase there is that *you are in charge.* Spence watching over the project is in line with office procedure. It's purely a we-need-to-know-what's-happening check. You know that."

"That was a lot of words," Ellie said in a stunned voice.

"I wanted to be clear."

This time, she rolled her eyes at him. "Uh-huh. You're sure you're not doing something else?"

Derrick smiled. "I have no idea what you're talking about."

Abby got it. Derrick rarely explained himself. He'd gone into an office-manual description with his answer. That immediately put Abby on edge. The idea of Derrick playing matchmaker or trying to push people together to talk…forget it. That was ridiculous. He wasn't that great with people, which is why his assistant, Jackson Richards, worked nonstop and everyone ran to him for everything.

It also explained why the entire office celebrated when Derrick fell in love with Ellie. Everyone hoped love would soften him. It had, except for the palpable panic that now hovered around him due to the endangered pregnancy.

Still, shortly after Spence left town, Abby had been promoted. She'd seriously considered turning the offer down out of fear of it being perceived as a payoff to get her to keep quiet about the Jameson men shenanigans. Then she decided she qualified for the position and needed the money because there was no way she was staying at Jameson for long.

She went from assistant to project manager. Now she had a seat at the manager's table. She didn't need a full-time babysitter, and certainly not *that* full-time babysitter. "Spence showed up at a site meeting unannounced."

"He does have access to your calendar," Derrick said.

Ellie patted Derrick's knee where it lay curled on the bed beside her. "I love you but you're not very good at this."

Loyalty. Derrick and Spence had it. Abby got that.

"No, it's fine." She tried to keep her voice even but knew she failed when Derrick frowned and Ellie's eyes widened.

"Really?" Ellie snorted. "Because that tone did not sound fine."

Derrick had stopped massaging Ellie's neck but he started again. "I think she's afraid she'll upset you if she launches into her why-I-hate-Spence speech."

Ellie waved the concern away as she turned the television from muted to off. "Nope. Jameson family gossip is ridiculously delicious. I'm always happy to hear it."

Hate Spence. If only. Abby's life would be so much easier if she did hate Spence. She'd tried. Her mind spun with all the ways he'd failed her. How he hadn't believed her or let her explain. She could call up a ton of hate for the elder Mr. Jameson and heaps of anger and disappointment for Spence, but that was it. And seeing him again…her normal breathing still hadn't returned.

She'd heard his deep, rich voice in the hallway at work and ducked into the closest office to avoid him. Then there was his face. That gorgeous face.

The straight black hair and striking light brown eyes. He'd been blessed with those extraordinary Jameson genes, including a hint of his Japanese grandmother around the nose and cheeks. Tall, almost six-two with impossibly long legs and a trim waist, Spence was a bit more muscled than Derrick. Spence's shoulders, and that pronounced collarbone, cried out for kisses.

Not that she noticed.

She was trying really hard not to notice.

With a shake, she forced her mind back to work and the best way to survive being in the same building as Spence. "Well, hopefully it was a one-time thing and I can submit reports or tell Jackson and make Jackson talk to Spence."

Derrick frowned. "That sounds like an efficient use of office resources."

"It might keep Spence alive." Ellie slipped her fingers through Derrick's as she spoke. "Just saying."

The gentle touch seemed to spark something in Derrick. He sat up a bit straighter as he looked at Abby. "If it's a problem to deal with Spence, I'll switch projects with him. I'll be the silent Jameson looming in the background on yours."

As if she could agree to that. Saying yes to the offer suggested she couldn't handle pressure, and that was not a message Abby wanted to send.

Ellie visibly squeezed his hand. "That's not really how you run the office, is it?"

"No," Derrick said.

Abby shrugged. "Sort of."

For a few seconds, no one spoke. They all looked

at each other, back and forth, as the tension rose. Abby wasn't clear on what was happening. Maybe some sort of unspoken chat between Ellie and Derrick. But Abby did know that the cool room suddenly felt suffocating. Even the cream-colored duvet cover with the tiny blue roses—an addition she would bet money moved in with Ellie—didn't ease the mood.

"Everything okay in here?" Spence's firm voice boomed into the silence.

He hovered right behind her. Abby could almost feel the heat pulse off his body. When he exhaled, his warm breath blew across the back of her neck.

Time to go. That phrase repeated in her head until it took hold.

"Spence." Ellie smiled. "Look, it's Spence."

"I do live here. Temporarily, but still."

In the bedroom down the hall. Abby knew because she'd walked by it a few days ago and glanced in. Saw a bag and hoped it meant nothing. Then she recognized Spence's tie from the day before flung over the unmade bed.

"For now." Abby meant to think and not say it, but she managed to mumble it.

Of course Spence heard and placed a hand on her lower back. "Meaning?"

The touch, perfectly respectable and so small, hit her like a live wire. Energy arced through her. She had to fight the urge to lean into him. To balance her body against his. "I'm sure you'll be on your way again soon."

Spence's exhale was louder, more dramatic this time. "That's not—"

Derrick stood up. "As fun as it is to see you two work things out by lobbing verbal volleys at each other, Ellie does need her rest."

"I'm having fun." Ellie caught Derrick's hand.

Abby silently thanked Derrick for giving her the easy out. Once she maneuvered her way through the three-story brick mansion, she'd be gone.

She put the box of brownies on the bed and pointed to them. "I just wanted to drop them off. Don't eat them all at once."

"You're very sweet." Ellie went to work on the tape holding the sides of the box down. "I make no promises about how fast they'll be gone." She shot Derrick and Spence a serious look. "So we're clear, I'm not sharing."

"No one would dare defy that order." Abby could not escape fast enough. "I'll text you later."

She pivoted around Spence and practically raced down the hall. Moved as fast as her stupid spiky heels would let her without wiping out in an inglorious sprawl. The humming in her head blocked out all sounds. She didn't realize she'd been followed until she reached the bottom of the intricately carved wooden staircase and heard footsteps behind her.

She turned around just as she left the steps. Spence was there. Of course he was.

With his palm flattened against the wall and his other on the banister, he stopped. She couldn't help but stare. His body was an amazing mystery to her. A package she ached to unwrap. How long were his arms, anyway?

His expression stayed blank as his gaze searched her face. "What are you doing here?"

"Visiting Ellie." Not a lie. She'd brought a treat and everything.

Spence finished coming down the stairs. Slipped his body by hers until they stood side by side. "How do you even know her?"

He still towered over her. She stood a good five-eight and with the heels could talk to anyone without feeling as if someone was trying to intimidate her. But Spence still towered, though he did stand a few steps back, giving her space.

"I do work at the company," she pointed out, not knowing what else to say.

"A lot of people work there. None of them show up at the boss's house." Spence folded his arms across his middle and stared her down. "What's really going on?"

He had to be kidding with this. "Do you think I'm stalking you?"

"Are you?"

She was doing the exact opposite, whatever that was called. Hiding from him? Sort of. Trying to find breathing room to center her control and ease the disappointment that clawed at her every time she thought about him and what could have been. "Lately, when I come over I text first to make sure you're gone. Happy?"

His arms slid down until they hung at his sides again. "Isn't that a bit extreme?"

"No." It was self-preservation.

She refused to get snared in another Jameson trap. She trusted Derrick. He'd delivered on every promise he'd made to her back then, when he begged her to stay with the company after...Spence.

"Sooner or later, we're going to need to talk to each other," Spence said.

"I disagree." Not her most mature answer ever but probably the most honest one.

"Abby, come on."

The tone of his voice suggested he was done playing games. Well, that made two of them. "It's fascinating that you ran off without saying a word months ago, but now you want some big chatty moment with me. I guess us talking is fine so long as it's convenient to you."

"We're adults."

Lecturing. Great. Just what she wanted from him. "One of us is."

With that, she turned and walked out. She'd reached her maximum load on Jameson testosterone for one day. She needed her shoes off and her feet up. Some wine. No Spence.

A Spence-free zone. The idea made her smile as she walked down the hall then closed the front door behind her.

* * *

"She's not wrong," Derrick said as he slowly walked down the stairs.

"You want to clue me in here?" Because Spence felt deflated and empty. The gnawing sensation refused to leave him. He'd blown out of the office all those months ago. Traveled around. Helped out on random building sites across the east. Lived a life so different from the spectacle he'd grown up in. All that competition. How his father pitted the three of them against each other. How Derrick always tried to protect them from Dad's wrath, especially Carter, the youngest.

They lost their mom to cancer. Their father didn't even have the decency to let her live out her life in peace. No, he moved her to a facility then marched in there one day and demanded a divorce so he could marry his mistress. He thought she was pregnant but she wasn't, so he quickly dumped the mistress, too. Then he ran through others. He was on wife number four and insisted this one had changed him. Yeah, right. The man treated women as disposable and his sons as property.

All that playing, all that acting at being a Big Man, and he let the business slide. Derrick had stepped in and saved it years ago. They all had to work there from the time they were teens. It was a family requirement, but Derrick was the one who rescued them all—including their father—and restored the family checking account when he took over the day-to-day operations four years ago.

That incredible turnaround was one of the reasons Spence stood on Derrick's first floor now. He owed Derrick. He also loved Derrick and wanted to help. That meant sticking around. Worse, it meant facing his demons and dealing with Abby.

Spence wasn't good at standing still. He'd always been the brother to keep moving. Go away to school. Go farther to a different school. Try to work somewhere else. Delay full-time work with the family as long as possible.

The Jameson name choked him. He didn't find it freeing or respectable. Forcing his feet to stay planted was taking all of his strength. He didn't have much left over to do battle with Abby.

"Are you admitting you're clueless? That's a start." The amusement was right there in Derrick's voice.

At the sound, some of the churning in Spence's gut eased. He had no idea how to handle Abby, but he could do the fake fighting-with-his-brother thing all day. "Don't make me punch you while your fiancée is on bed rest. She shouldn't see you beg and cry right now."

"Are you quoting from a dream you once had? Because that's not reality."

They'd physically fought only once. It was years ago, over their mother. Spence had been desperate to keep her in the house with nurses. Derrick, barely in his twenties, had tried to make it happen but couldn't. Spence had needed an outlet for his rage and Derrick was right there. The perfect target.

There was an almost three-year age difference between them, but Spence still got his ass kicked. And he'd deserved it because his anger really should have been aimed at his father. Spence was thirty-three now. In theory, he knew better.

"Spence, she's one of the best we have." Derrick sat down on a step a few from the bottom and started counting out Abby's attributes on his fingers. "She can multitask and oversee projects, keep things moving. She's smart. She's a great negotiator."

It was an impressive list, but Spence already knew it by heart. Every time he tried to run through her sins in his mind, the image of her face would pop up and his thoughts would stumble. "I feel like you're reading her résumé to me."

"Don't scare her away."

There was no amusement in his tone now. Spence got the message. "You do understand she screwed me, right?"

"I don't know what happened back then because you bolted and when I tried to talk with her, in part to make sure we weren't going to get sued, she refused to say one single negative thing about you." Derrick threw up his hands before balancing them on his thighs again. "Hell, I can name twenty bad things just sitting here and without thinking very hard, but she protected you."

"She sure has no problem listing out my faults now."

"Do you hear what I'm saying?"

"That you're nosy as hell." Spence dropped down on the step two down from Derrick and stretched out sideways so he could look at Derrick. "What's your actual point?"

"Maybe you got it wrong back then."

Spence leaned his head back against the staircase railing and stared up at the ceiling. "I saw her kissing Dad."

"Right, because our father never set anyone up or did anything to mess with us."

That got Spence's attention. His head lowered and he looked at Derrick. "I don't—"

"When rumors were going around about me in an attempt to convince Ellie to dump me, Abby's name came up."

"What?"

"Some people think the two of us had a thing. There are whispers, none of them true, but they're out there." Derrick shrugged. "Ellie heard, wanted to apologize to Abby for dragging her into our personal mess, they met and, honestly, it's like they've known each other for years."

Derrick and Abby. Fake or not, there was an image Spence never wanted in his head. But Abby and Ellie? No one was safe if those two put their powers together. "That's just great."

"For you, no. Abby is going to be around here for Ellie. And she's a big part of the managerial team at work." Derrick dropped his arm and touched the step right by Spence's shoulder. "I want you here and I will do anything to keep you in the office and in town, but even I can't work miracles. You have to fix this because I can't."

"I've never heard you admit that before."

"You're going to run into her."

Derrick sounded so serious. Spence wanted to make a joke or ignore the whole conversation. He knew he couldn't do either. "I can handle it."

"I'm wondering if the rest of us will survive it."

Suddenly, so was Spence.

Three

Abby sat in a conference room on the fifteenth floor of the swanky office building where Jameson Industries was located. A glass wall with the glass door fronted the room, facing into the hall. The room was reserved for relatively few people in the company because it connected to Jackson Richards's office next door. He used it. Derrick used it. Today, she used it.

She looked at the stack of papers in front of her, then to her laptop, then across the small round table to Jackson. He was Derrick's right-hand man and the most accessible person on the management staff. He was also tall and lean with a runner's body and, if rumors were correct, the one every single woman in the office named as the most eligible and interesting man in the office. There hadn't been an actual poll, to her knowledge, but she got asked at least a few times a week if he was dating anyone. Not that Abby saw him in a romantic way. She didn't.

She considered Jackson one of her closest friends, if not *the* closest. After a relatively solitary existence growing up—just her and her mom and the apartment manager who watched her when her mom worked the night shift at the diner—dating here and there, keeping attachments light in case she needed to get up and go, Jackson acted as a lifeline for her. They even lived in condos next door to each other, which was more of an accident than anything else. But when you heard about a good deal on a downtown DC property with a doorman and reasonable monthly fees, you jumped on it. Jackson sure had.

But right now she was at work and out of patience. She beat back the urge to knock her head against the table. "If I have to read one more email from Rylan, my brain will explode."

The man sent her the most mundane emails. The status check today, which he sent a day earlier than he said he would, was to tell her nothing had changed. Yeah, she guessed that much. But with emails clogging her inbox and her mind on constant wandering mode these days, she needed something solid. Jackson was it.

"Good thing we have good health insurance here," Jackson said as he closed the file he was reading.

She snorted. "I'm pretty sure head explosion isn't covered."

"He is persistent." Jackson glanced at the conference room door as it opened. "Speaking of which…"

"Hello." Spence stepped inside. He didn't make a move to sit down. He stopped and rested his palms on the back of the chair nearest to him.

That fast, the oxygen sucked out of the room. The easy banter with Jackson gave way to suffocating tension. It pressed in on Abby, proving what she already knew. Seeing Spence grew harder each time, not easier.

Jackson smiled as he moved some of the files and papers around to make room in front of an open chair. "Hey, Spence."

As far as Abby was concerned, all of that accommodating was unnecessary. She had no interest in sitting there, explaining her projects to Spence. She had a file made up with the relevant information and emailed him the rest. She'd done her part to keep the machine running.

"Right." She shut her laptop, careful not to slam the cover down, and stood up. "I'm going to head back to my office."

"I need to talk to you for a second." Spence's gaze moved from her to Jackson.

Jackson sighed. "Why are you looking at me? I'm supposed to be in here. I'm not leaving."

"Help me out," Spence said.

Jackson shook his head as he stood up. "Did you not hear my dramatic sigh?"

"It was tough to miss."

"That's because I spend half my life rescuing Jamesons from certain disaster." Jackson ended the back-and-forth with a smack against Spence's shoulder.

Some of the tension drained away as Jackson and Spence fell into their easy camaraderie. That sort of thing always amazed Abby. Men could argue and go at each other, but if they were friends or related, they seemed to have this secret signal, heard only by them, that triggered the end of the battle. Then all the anger slipped away.

She wished she possessed that skill.

She glanced at Jackson. "You deserve a raise."

"Hell, yeah." Jackson winked at her as he walked out of the conference room through the connecting door to his office.

A second later, Spence slid into the seat Jackson abandoned. He flipped through a whole repertoire of nervous gestures, none of which she'd seen from him before. He rubbed the back of his neck. Shifted around in his seat. Put a hand on the table then took it off. But he didn't say a word.

After about a minute, the silence screamed in her head. "You're up, Spence. You're the one who wanted to talk."

Fight was probably more accurate. They couldn't seem to be civil to each other for more than a few minutes at a time since living in the same town again. They verbally sparred. Every conversation led them back to the same place—he believed she came on to his father. The idea made her want to heave.

He let out a heavy sigh that had his chest lifting and falling. "We got off on the wrong foot."

"When?"

He frowned. "What?"

"Now or back then?" She was having a hard time keeping up, so he was going to need to be more specific. "Maybe when we were starting to go out and had plans for our first official date that Friday. You left on Thursday without a word."

The memories flashed in her brain and she blinked them out. She refused to let the sharp pain in her chest derail her. This close, right across the table, she could see the intensity in his eyes, smell that scent she associated with him. A kind of peppery sharpness that reeled her in. In the past. Not now. She wouldn't let it happen now.

"You are determined to make this difficult." He had the nerve to look wounded.

She pushed down her anger and lifted her chin. "Do you blame me?"

"Actually, yes." He sat back in the chair. The metal creaked under his weight as he lifted the front two legs off the floor. "You kissed my father."

And there it was. The only point he could make, so he did it over and over until it lost its punch. "So you've pointed out. Repeatedly."

"Okay. Enough." A thud echoed through the small room as the front legs of his chair hit the floor again.

"I agree." She stood up. Her vision blurred. She struggled through a haze of anger and disappointment to see the stacks of documents and folders in front of her.

"Please, sit." His hand slipped over hers. "I know

you think I'm an ass, but I'm here because I am worried about Ellie and the baby. The chance of my big brother running himself into the ground is really good. He may be acting cool, but he's a panicked mess."

Part of her wanted to throw his hand off hers. The other part wanted to grab hold. Her life would have been so much easier if she could have hated him. She begged the universe to let that happen.

Instead, she slipped her hand out from under his, stopped moving her things around and looked at him. "Of course he is. He loves Ellie."

Spence's gaze traveled over her face. "You like Derrick."

All the blood ran out of her head. "You're not accusing me—"

"No!" Spence held up both hands as if in mock surrender. "I mean, respect. Friendship. Deeper than a boss, but not romantic."

Her heartbeat stopped thundering in her ears. It was as if he opened his mouth and her body prepared for battle. The whole thing gave her a headache. "That's fair. Yes."

"Any chance we could get there? I'd like us to be friends." His hand rested on the table, so close to hers.

She stared at his long fingers. She'd always loved his hands. They showed strength. Seeing them made her wonder what they would feel like on her.

She pushed the thought away. "No."

"Abby, come on."

"I have that level of trust and understanding with Derrick because there is nothing else in the way. Nothing else between us because I don't have any other feelings for him." The words echoed in her head. She closed her eyes for a second before opening them again, hoping she'd only thought them. But no, there he was. Staring at her. Clear that he heard every syllable.

His eyebrow lifted. "But you do feel something for me?"

The look on his face. Was that satisfaction or hope? She couldn't tell. Didn't want to know. She never meant to open that door. Thinking it and saying it were two very different things, and she'd blown it. Now she rushed to try to fix the damage. "Did. That's over."

"Is it?"

He stood up then. Took one step toward her. Not too close, but enough to cut off her breathing. To make her fight not to gasp.

"I want to kiss you." He put his hands on her arms and turned her slightly until they faced each other. "Tell me no if you don't want me to."

They'd kissed before. Gone to dinner, stolen a few minutes in closed conference rooms now and then. But this one was lined with windows on one side. She looked over his shoulder, thinking someone would be out there. That her brain would click on and common sense would come rushing back. For once, no one rushed up and down the hall.

She opened her mouth to say no, sensing he actually would stop. But she couldn't get the word out. Not that one. "Yes."

With the unexpected green light, he leaned in. His mouth covered hers and need shot through her. The press of his mouth, the sureness of his touch. His lips didn't dance over hers. They didn't test or linger. No, this was the kind of kiss where you dove in and held on.

His mouth slipped over hers and her knees buckled. She grabbed on to the sleeve of his shirt. Dug her fingers into the material as desire pounded her. Her brain shut down and her body took over. She wanted to wrap her legs around his and slip her fingers through that sexy dark hair.

Voices in the hallway floated through her. She heard laughter and the mumbling. The noise broke the spell.

"Stop." She pushed away from him. Still held on but lessened her grip and put a bit of air between them. "Don't."

Her gaze went back to the glass wall. She heard talking but didn't see anyone. Not unusual at this end of the hall since only Derrick and Jackson had offices there. But she took the sound of voices as a warning. Forcing her fingers to uncurl, she dropped her arms and stepped back another step, ignoring the way the corner of her chair jammed into the side of her thigh.

"Sorry." Spence visibly swallowed. "I know I'm your boss and it's weird."

She looked at him then. Really looked. Saw the flush on his cheeks and his swollen lips. That haze clouding his eyes. He had been as spun up and knocked off balance as she was. It was tempting to shut it all down and let him believe this was about Human Resources and office rules, but it wasn't. Employees could date and this wasn't about that.

"We both know this isn't workplace harassment. You asked permission and I said yes. I know my job doesn't depend on kissing you. There's no big power play here." She laid a lot of sins at his feet, but not that one. His father? Yes. But not Spence.

"I guess that's something."

"You hated me and ran away but never threatened my job. You're not that guy." She waved a hand between them. "But this—us—we've proven it doesn't work. We're miserable around each other."

"I never hated you."

No way was she going to dissect that and examine it. "Okay."

"And are we? You make me feel a lot of things, Abby. Miserable isn't one of them."

And she was ignoring that, too. She had to. Believing, even for a second, that he might trust her, that he might get what he did when he sided with his father months ago, was too dangerous. He'd been clear about what he thought of her back then. They needed to stick with that and stay away from each other.

She grabbed her laptop. Almost dropped it. "I need to prep for another meeting with Rylan."

Spence watched the fumbling. Even tried to help when the laptop started its dive, but when she pulled it all together, he stepped back again. Slipped his hands in his pants pockets. "When is it? I'll come with you."

"To the meeting? Do you think I can't handle it?" He really was determined to babysit her. Thinking about that killed off her need to unbutton his shirt and strip it off him. Mostly.

"That guy's interest in you is not entirely professional."

Her brain cells scrambled. She didn't understand what he was saying or why now. "And you're worried I'll kiss him, too?"

"I'm concerned he won't know where the line is. I don't want you to be put in an untenable position." Whatever he saw on her face had him frowning. "What?"

"Where was this Spence months ago?" She would have done anything to have him stick up for her then. To be on her side.

"What does that mean?"

She retreated back behind her safe wall. Her mother had taught her to be wary. She'd learned the hard way from the man who never stuck around to be a dad. Then her mom taught the ultimate lesson when she died in that diner shooting. Abby had to be stronger, smarter. Always be ready. Always be careful.

"I'll be fine." Somehow, she made her legs move. The shaking in her hands had her laptop bouncing against her chest from the death grip she had on it. She ignored all of it, and Spence, as she walked out.

But that kiss she would remember.

* * *

Spence couldn't forget the kiss or that look on Abby's face. It was as if she expected him not to believe her, not to stick up for her. Then his mind slipped back to another office. Another kiss. He'd walked in and his life had turned upside down. All that hatred for his father manifested itself in one horrible second, and he'd taken it out on Abby. She knew about his father's charm and his effect on women. He'd just hoped she would be different.

That realization brought him to Derrick's office. Spence didn't want to talk, but hanging out with Derrick generally calmed him. He was a reminder that the Jameson men could turn out to be decent. Their grandfather was a disgraced congressman. Dad was considered a big-time successful businessman who always had a beautiful woman on his arm. Spence and his brothers had spent too much time in the public eye as props for family photos and public relations schemes.

But Derrick was the real thing. He didn't see it, but Carter and Spence did.

As soon as Spence walked in, Derrick motioned for him to take the seat on the other side of his massive desk. Without saying a word, Derrick opened the top drawer and took out a large envelope. "Here."

Spence wasn't exactly looking for work talk but he sensed that's not what this was anyway. "Do I want to know what this is?"

"It's from Dad."

The damn agreement. Despite all of Derrick's

hard work, Eldrick owned the majority of the company. He promised to turn it over, but not before he put his boys through another set of tests. It was his way of holding on to power and exerting control.

Derrick had been given a specific time to clean up his reputation. He was also supposed to lure Carter and Spence home, which proved easy enough once Derrick admitted it to them. But he did more than that. He managed to run a multimillion-dollar company, expand its holding, meet their father's conditions and land the best woman for him.

For Derrick—easy. For anyone else? Likely impossible.

Spence hated to guess what his task was. "Lucky me."

Derrick dropped the envelope on the desk. "Rip it up without opening it."

The suggestion didn't make sense. "What?"

"Walk away from this."

"Isn't this my stipulation, the things I have to do? The way you explained it to me before, Dad only turns over the business if we all do his bidding. You had the biggest part and finished. Now it's my turn." Still, Spence couldn't bring himself to touch the envelope.

"Don't let him do this. It's manipulation."

It was. No one debated that. Not the lawyers who drew up the documents. Not Jackson, the only person outside of the family who knew other than Ellie. The requirements were personal and not likely to be legally enforceable, but with controlling interest, dear old Dad could sell the company and take the company that meant everything to Derrick away from him at any time. Spence refused to let that happen, even if it meant staying and working there.

"You deserve to run the company. You saved it." To Spence, it was that simple. He'd talked to Carter, their younger, California-living brother. He agreed with Spence. Whatever it took to beat the old man and get Derrick the business, they would do it.

Derrick shrugged. "I'll find another way."

"I'm thinking it's time I stepped up and took responsibility." Something even Spence had to admit he should have done before. Stopped running long enough to help.

"Are we only talking about the job?" Derrick smiled as he asked the question.

"This isn't about Abby." It was infuriating how she was the first thing that popped into his mind—always. Spence couldn't kick that habit.

"Right, Abby." Derrick made a humming sound. "Do you notice how you brought up her name, not me?"

Spence was not touching that. He knew he had a weakness for her. There was no need to pretend otherwise. "I was talking about being more engaged here, at work."

Derrick sat back in his chair. "I can't say I hate that idea."

"Yeah, well, don't get excited. I might suck at it."

This time, Derrick laughed. He'd so rarely done that in the past, but he did it now that he'd found Ellie. "I like the positive attitude."

Spence never had one of those before. Maybe it was time he tried. "I'm being realistic."

"I'll take whatever I can get."

Four

Abby kicked off her high heels and dropped down on her sectional sofa. Next, she propped her feet up on the round leather ottoman in front of her. If she had the energy, she'd change out of her work clothes. She picked dropping her head back against the cushions and closing her eyes instead.

The condo was on the seventh floor of a secure-building that sat a block off of Logan Circle. The trendy area became trendy during the last decade. Now galleries and restaurants and fitness studios lined the streets. Several parks nearby provided great places to run and bike, but she tried never to do either. She preferred walking the city and turning her muscles to mush in kickboxing classes.

She picked the building because of the location.

She was able to get in on the newly refurbished space before the prices skyrocketed and used a work bonus to do it. Now she laughed when she heard what people were willing to pay for studios on lower floors in the building. It was an odd feeling when the place you lived became a place you likely could no longer afford if you were trying to buy *right now*.

There were four condos per floor and those were serviced by a private elevator. A penthouse stretched the full length of the building on the floor above but there was never any noise up there except when the couple who lived there threw one of their lavish rooftop garden parties. She'd never been invited but she loved sitting out on her tiny balcony and listening to the music and laughter as it spun through the DC night.

The best part of the building was her neighbor—Jackson. His two-bedroom also had a den. She didn't need the extra space or the bigger price tag, but she loved having him close by. The man appreciated takeout. One of his many fine attributes.

The door opened after a quick knock. She didn't get up because she didn't have to. She'd texted Jackson as she walked in the door. She wanted Chinese food and could almost always convince him to share with her.

"You're drinking wine already?" He laughed as he relaxed into the corner seat of her sectional.

She opened her eyes and looked at him. He'd stripped off his tie and rolled up the sleeves of his shockingly white dress shirt. His hair showed signs that he'd run his fingers through it repeatedly during the day.

He really was attractive. Those big eyes and the athletic build. Decent and smart. Hardworking and compassionate. Funny. And she felt nothing but a big loving friendship for him.

Clearly there was something wrong with her. She knew what it was and didn't try to hide it. "Spence."

"Ah." Jackson reached behind him to the table that sat there. "Here's the bottle."

Abby watched Jackson fill a glass for himself then put the bottle on a wooden tray on the ottoman for easy reach. If they were going to talk about Spence, and they were because she needed to blow off some of the frustration pinging around inside of her, then she might need a second glass.

She skipped over the kissing part of the afternoon and how that rocked her so hard she'd spent the rest of the day brushing her fingertips over her lips. "He talks and I want to punch him in the face."

"That sounds like a healthy reaction."

She ran her fingers up and down the stem of her glass. "Doesn't it make you frustrated, having to deal with the Jamesons and their money and power and bullying behavior?"

His eyebrow lifted. "Are we still talking about work?"

"He makes me…" She couldn't even find the right word. Hot, angry, spun up, frustrated. They all fit.

"Want to punch him." Jackson toasted her with his glass. "Yeah, I got it."

"I love Ellie. She's funny and smart and charming and doesn't take their crap."

"Sounds like someone else I know." When she frowned, he kept talking. "It does. You don't get onto the managerial team at a family-owned company unless you're good. You're damn good."

"Like you?" She knew the truth. Jackson was a star at work. Derrick depended on him. Everyone did. Even she did. If you needed an answer, he likely had it.

He acted as if he were thinking something over. "Maybe I do deserve a raise."

"I'm tired of all of it."

"Wait." He put down his glass, took hers and did the same with it. "That sounds suspiciously like you're thinking about finding a new job and leaving."

She felt a little lost without the glass to grab on to and started talking with her hands. "Don't you toy with the idea? Leave, open your own place. Do some consulting."

"Sounds risky but potentially rewarding, except for the part where you'll work round the clock, be panicked about finances and eat peanut butter for every meal so you can stockpile cash." He shook his head. "I've already lived that life. I really don't want to go back."

They shared a similar background, having been raised by single moms who barely earned enough money to keep the lights on. But he hadn't been alone. He had a sister, a twin. But it had just been Abby. She depended on her mom until the day she lost her, and she'd mourned her every day since. Missed the vanilla-scented shampoo she used. Her smile. The way she laughed at bad horror movies. That loss, so deep and raw, never disappeared. Moving forward became easier but was never easy.

But this was about her, and her work life and figuring out the best choice for her, separate from the Spence piece of the puzzle. "Me, either, but I'm not afraid of putting in the hours."

"I don't doubt you at all." Jackson studied her for a second before picking up her wineglass and handing it to her again. "Not to bring up a rough subject, but you know Eldrick is coming to town, right?"

Spence's dad. Abby despised the man.

"What?" The glass slipped in her hands and wine splashed over the side and dribbled down her hand. She caught it before it hit her light gray couch or her silk blouse.

"I had a feeling you didn't know."

"Are you sure it's happening?" Because that was her nightmare. Dealing with Spence was rough. Not smashing a computer over Eldrick's head might prove impossible.

He'd left shortly after he'd kissed her all those months ago, made it clear he did it to teach Spence a lesson. Since then, he'd married another wife and left the country. Abby seethed every day since. She'd hoped he'd stay on that beach in Tortola forever, but no such luck.

"Found out today." Jackson kept watching her, as if he were assessing if he should shut up or provide more details. "It's for Ellie and Derrick's engagement party. They postponed it when Ellie fainted and figured out she was pregnant. Derrick told his dad to stay away, but now the shindig is back on and father Jameson is flying in with the newest wife."

"Ever met her?"

"No, but Derrick had her investigated, so I learned too much." Jackson made a you-don't-want-to-know face.

Abby rolled her eyes. "Of course he did."

"The Jameson men are somewhat predictable."

"It's scary."

"Eldrick Jameson is…" Jackson made a humming sound. "I can't actually think of a decent thing to say about that man."

"Me, either. But go back a second. Ellie is still on bed rest." Abby didn't want her friend confined, but she didn't want a reason to see Eldrick, either.

"I don't think that means we tie her to the bed and keep her there. She's allowed to move."

"But a party? Isn't that stressful?" It would be for Abby.

"They're being extra careful." Jackson shrugged. "Getting the doctor's okay and all that. Trust me, Derrick isn't happy about it, either. I think after all the rumors in the paper about them, Ellie wants the party to stop any whispers."

That meant this was happening. It sounded like Derrick was throwing up roadblocks but none of them showed any promise in stopping the party. "Ugh."

Jackson laughed. "I can hear the excitement in your voice."

He might as well have said *funeral*. "I hate parties. Derrick hates parties."

"But he loves her."

That made Abby smile. "They really are too cute. I mean it. *Too* cute."

"Well, if it's any consolation, they were a mess at first. Derrick nearly blew it about a hundred times." Jackson shook his head. "It was kind of pathetic."

"Maybe there's some relationship malfunction in the Jameson gene pool."

Jackson drained his glass and poured another. "I've often thought that."

"I'm supposed to go over and see Ellie at lunch tomorrow." Abby wanted to cancel, or at least get some sort of promise that Spence would not show up. He seemed to be doing that a lot these days.

"Business?"

"Girl talk."

Jackson made a face. "Do I want to know what that means?"

"I don't know." It wasn't exactly Abby's strength, either. She'd grown up with few friends and kept that streak going most of her life. That's why when Ellie took her in and insisted they get to know each other, and then introduced her to her best friend, Vanessa, Abby didn't balk. She took the risk this one time and it had paid off. Spending time with Ellie made Abby smile. "She texted. I'm going."

"The things we do to make the pregnant woman happy."

Abby lifted her near-empty glass. "I'll toast to that."

The next afternoon, Abby arrived at Ellie's house, weighed down with bags of food. Derrick had to go into work for a few meetings, so Abby used the code and slipped through the layers of security to get inside. Then up the stairs. A few minutes later, she unloaded the salads and caprese-on-focaccia sandwiches onto the tray set up on the edge of Ellie's bed with drinks and what looked like a bowl of pretzels.

Ellie sat propped up in the chair next to the bed with her legs stretched out on the ottoman in front of her. Abby guessed she wasn't on the bed because it was covered with envelopes and papers.

"The sandwiches smelled so good on the walk over from the deli that I almost ate one." Abby pushed some of the paperwork to the side and sat on the edge of the bed. "What is all this?"

Ellie smiled as she grabbed a sandwich out of the bag. "It's party time. Two and a half weeks."

"Really?" Abby tried to keep the dread out of her voice but she was pretty sure it seeped in. "You know you're supposed to be in bed, right?"

"The doctor gave the okay. I have to sit for most of it, some of it with my feet up, which is really boring. The party has to be in the afternoon and not long." Ellie unwrapped the paper and ripped off a piece of focaccia. "I'm pretty sure Derrick will carry around a timer and make sure I don't stand for more than three minutes at a time."

"Because that sounds reasonable."

"He's ridiculous." But a huge grin formed on Ellie's lips as she shrugged. "It's kind of adorable."

"I'm surprised he didn't fire the doctor and find one who forbids parties." Abby felt bad that the idea sounded so good to her. "The man is not a great socializer."

"As opposed to you."

She had to cut this off. Spence was going to be Ellie's brother-in-law, which meant whining about him would put her in a terrible position. Abby didn't want to do that. "We're not talking about Spence."

Ellie's hands dropped to her lap and her smile grew even wider...if that was possible. "Look how you jumped right to him. Interesting."

"Don't make me grab the food and run." Abby took her time digging around in the bag, looking for a napkin.

"That's just mean." Ellie barely let the words sit there before she launched into her next point. "But I would say—"

"Oh, here we go." Abby gave up. She could only fake interest in the inside of a bag for so long before it seemed weird, and she feared she was nearing that line. "I'm listening."

She also twisted the paper napkin between her fingers. In, out and around. Tight enough that she heard the paper rip.

"The sparks between you two? Whoa."

Oh, man. That couldn't be true. She'd tried so hard to hide it, to fight it off.

Abby refolded the mangled napkin, then turned to the sandwich. Unwrapped each edge. But the grumbling in her stomach from before had vanished. This topic seemed to zap the hunger right out of her.

She dumped the uneaten sandwich on the tray next to her. "What you're sensing? That's anger."

"Babe, I know anger. That is not what I see." Ellie took a bite, then another.

"We may have some...unresolved issues."

"The queen of understatement."

Yeah, no kidding. But that led to a bigger issue, one Abby was not totally sure how to discuss. "I need you to know that I might not be at the engagement party."

"Wrong." Ellie smiled and reached for her bottle of water. "But why are you under that incorrect assumption?"

Abby tried to pick up anger, anything in Ellie's voice that suggested disappointment. She sounded more resigned to prove Abby wrong than anything else.

"Those unresolved issues relate to Papa Jameson and—"

"The kiss?" Ellie's eyebrow lifted. "Yeah, I don't blame you there. My father-in-law-to-be deserves a good kick."

Apparently there was an office memo no one bothered to tell her about. As far as Abby knew, Derrick had kept the kiss information limited to a very few in the office. The idea that someone other than a small circle and Ellie might know made Abby's stomach roll. She didn't want to be viewed as someone who lied and schemed her way to the top. She didn't care what choices other people made, but she'd earned this position by working her butt off.

Abby picked up the napkin then put it down again. "You know about that?"

"Of course. It's the kiss heard 'round the family." Ellie looked at Abby's face and her smile disappeared. She waved a hand and shook her head. "No, don't panic. Actually, I made Derrick tell me, but he wasn't all that forthcoming with juicy details. All I know is Spence thinks you were playing a power game and kissed his dad."

Abby's stomach refused to stop somersaulting. If this kept up, she could forget about lunch because she'd be seeing her breakfast again. "He's an idiot."

"Which one?"

And that's why she liked Ellie so much. "Good point. Both of them."

Ellie winced. "I haven't met father Jameson yet."

"Lucky you."

"How bad was it back then?"

Intolerable. All hands and creepy looks. Word was Spence's father liked to pick interns by their looks— young, pretty and blonde. A practice Derrick immediately stopped once he figured it out. But there was no reason to completely terrify Ellie during her shaky pregnancy. "Bad enough that I'm considering skipping a party and missing cake, which is sacred food in my book."

"If I let you punch him, will you come?" Ellie sounded excited by the idea.

So was Abby. "Which him?"

"Either. Both."

So tempting. "That might be a deal I can't pass up."

"Believe it or not, I really like Spence," Ellie said.

Some of Abby's amusement faded. "Let's not go there."

"Of course, I've only know him for a few weeks."

"I worked with him, was wildly attracted to him. Fought it off and lost. And then I *really* lost." That was more than Abby usually admitted. Jackson knew pieces of the story and a bit about her feelings, about how hurt and torn apart she'd been. Derrick had made it clear back then he'd collected some of the facts but not all of them. It didn't matter because Abby didn't want to relive any of it.

"Any chance Spence can redeem himself?" Ellie asked.

Abby had asked herself that a thousand times over the last few months. She dreamed about Spence showing up and apologizing. Ran through all these scenarios on what she would say. But Spence stole that opportunity away from her, too, because he never came back for her. He came back for Derrick and Ellie. Abby vowed not to forget that.

She cleared her throat, swallowing back the lump that had formed there. "I have to be smarter than that, more self-protective this time around."

The memory of the kiss flashed in her mind. Not the one that destroyed everything. The one from yesterday. The new one that carried a note of hope and a hint of desperation. The feelings had thrummed off Spence. And she'd been trying to forget them, talk herself out of the way her heart leaped and her body turned all mushy when his lips touched hers, ever since.

Ellie shook her head. "Men. They do ruin things sometimes."

Abby suddenly felt like eating again. "No kidding."

Five

She'd ignored him for three days. Spence wasn't great about being shut out of anything. He also didn't trust Rylan, and that's exactly who Abby was meeting with today. Right now.

The door stood open. Papers were strewn across the conference room table. Maps and documents with official government seals. A thick binder filled with information Spence knew would bore him.

Spence waited until the last minute to slip into the room she'd reserved for the meeting. Rylan stood by the window, looking down into the street. The only noise in the room came from the sound of the automatic room fan. That and the squeak of Abby's chair as she moved it back and forth while studying the paper in front of her.

She glanced up as soon as the door clicked shut. "You're sitting in on all of my meetings now?"

The refusal to back down... Spence found that so sexy. "I actually work here."

She treated him to the perfect eye roll. It almost shouted *you're a jerk.* "For now."

Spence kept walking until he got to her side. Then he slid into the seat next to her with his arm resting on the table. "This idea you have that I'm ready to bolt? Get it out of your head. It's not happening."

She slowly lowered her pen. "It did before."

Shot landed. Spence felt it vibrate through him. The truth really did suck sometimes.

"Derrick needs me here." That was also true. He'd come back for his brother and his growing family. Spence had repeated that to himself during the entire journey to DC. Now he wondered if something else pulled him there. An invisible thread that bound him to Abby. A need to come home and resolve the seemingly unresolvable.

She tapped her pen end over end against the table. The clicking sound turned to a steady thump when she started to hit it harder. "And no one needed you before?"

"Didn't feel like it." He'd felt betrayed, yet not. Almost as if he'd expected Abby to disappoint him back then.

Man, that was not something he wanted to examine too closely. At least not there, in an office conference room.

Rylan picked that moment to turn around and face the room. "Is everything okay between you two?"

Abby lifted her hand without looking in Rylan's direction. "You remember Rylan."

"Hard to forget." Rylan was the kind of guy who lingered. Maybe not dangerous but not honest, either. Spence knew the other man was stringing the approval process out. He was either receiving a payment from a competing company under the table, or he had a crush on Abby. Spence hated both options. "Do we have the final okay to proceed?"

Rylan stepped up to the table. "Soon."

A pounding started at the base of the back of Spence's neck. "What does that mean?"

Rylan's mouth opened and closed a few times before he actually stumbled and got a few words out. "There is still some work to be done."

Ah, work. Sure. "Then why are you here instead of off doing it?"

Rylan glanced at Abby but she just smiled at him. That told Spence that she was sick of the stalling, too.

"This is a status meeting," Rylan finally said.

"Didn't you two meet about a week ago?" Spence leaned back in his chair, enjoying the line of sweat that appeared on Rylan's forehead. "I'm asking but, see, I know that answer because I was there."

"I also needed to deliver some documents to Abby." Rylan picked his briefcase off the floor and took out a white envelope. He handed it to her without breaking eye contact with Spence.

She took it and tucked it into her file. "Thank you."

Since she wasn't balking at his heavy-handed behavior, Spence figured he had the green light to continue. Rylan stood frozen with his hand on the back of one of the chairs. He didn't make a move to sit down or do anything that looked like work.

"And now you can go." Spence made the words sound like an order.

It worked because Rylan took off on a frenzy of activity. He loaded up his briefcase and reached for his suit jacket. He nearly tripped over his own feet getting to the door. "I'll call you as soon as I have the answers you need."

The door slammed behind him. Then Spence was alone with Abby. He hoped this round would go better than the last few. Except for the kiss. He'd be happy to repeat that.

Abby flicked the pen back and forth between her fingers. She seemed calm, maybe even a little amused.

Spence was smart enough to know quiet sometimes meant dangerous. He seriously considered ducking.

She waited a few more minutes, drawing out the tension and letting it build before she talked. That pen kept twirling in the air. "Is your plan to walk into every meeting I have and bully people?"

The tone. So judging. "Have you always been this dramatic?"

She eyed him up. "Yesterday you sat in on a meeting at the office and never said a word."

He suddenly felt sorry for the people who worked under her. She knew how to use that voice, that look, to set the tone. No one had to guess her mood. "I'm confused. You want me to talk, then you don't."

"It made people uncomfortable."

He knew the feeling. "You mean you?"

The invisible hold pulling between them broke. She looked away as she shook her head. "Your ego is amazing."

"Thank you." He stretched his arm out along the table. Almost touched her but was smart enough not to try. "About Rylan."

She straightened up the stack of papers in front of her. "We need him to sign off on a variety of environmental issues. He's dragging his feet, but it will happen. You know that."

So professional. Every word was true. That's how the process worked, but Spence was talking about something very different. He sensed she knew that. "And you know he's interested in more than hazardous waste."

"He's still within a reasonable time frame for getting the work done."

An interesting answer. One he decided to hit head-on. "Are you ignoring his crush in order to smooth the way for our approvals?"

"You didn't actually accuse me of using my looks to get what I want, so I'll let that pass." She stood up.

"I'm not a total jerk, Abby. I'm concerned that

he's making you uncomfortable or that he's harassing you. Neither is okay." Not liking the way it felt to sit while she loomed over him, he stood up, too. Kept his distance, or as much as being around the corner from each other at the table would allow. "I don't want him crossing a line."

Her eyes narrowed. It looked like she was studying him, trying to figure out if he was lying or not. "Women in the workplace have to maneuver through a labyrinth of ridiculous male behavior to get things done. But I have hard limits. I don't sleep around to get what I want."

The words struck right at the heart of their issues, but that's not where he was going, and digging into the past would only shut down the conversation. "I wasn't suggesting that."

"You did before."

He could not go back over that ground one more time. Part of him wanted to forgive and forget and move on. He didn't know if he could, but he was sure she was not up for the "forget" part. "Abby."

She went back to the papers. Stacked and restacked the same group twice before looking up at him again. "I'm just making my position clear since you think this has been an issue for me in the past. Don't want to be wrongly accused again."

"You'll tell me if you need me to—"

"That's the thing, Spence." She dropped the papers she was holding and they fell against the table with a whoosh. "You can't swoop in and fix this."

"First, I do not swoop."

She snorted. "If you say so."

"Second, I don't want any woman in this office to deal with nonsense." And he meant that. The last few generations of Jameson men had issues with women. He was determined to break the cycle and he knew Derrick and Carter wanted that, too.

"That last part is a responsible and appropriate thing for a boss to say, and maybe even a little sweet, but it's also impossible. There will always be some level of nonsense."

The words deflated him. "I'm sorry."

"For?"

The list was so damn long and went far beyond the topic they were discussing. "Everything? I'm really not sure, but I hate this feeling. The wall between us. The anger. The broken trust."

She blew out a long breath. "It's in the past. We should let it go."

He knew that made sense but it sounded wrong. They kept going at each other, but under all that anger, all the frustration and disappointment, something else lingered. Something he wasn't ready to let go of. "What if I don't want it to stay in the past? We could go over it now."

The color left her face. "Sometimes you need to move on."

"And sometimes you need to stick around and fix things." He stepped in closer and took her hands in his.

"You're saying…"

He wasn't even sure. "Finish the sentence."

His thumb rubbed over the backs of her hands. A light caress over her smooth skin. Then his hand slipped up. To her wrist, then a bit higher. Fingers on bare skin.

She jerked away, pulling back and putting space between them again. Her hands visibly shook as she grabbed for her files and her phone. "Thanks for the offer of help with Rylan, but I've got this."

He thought about stopping her, but now wasn't the time. When she walked out the door, leaving it hanging wide-open behind her, he wondered if the time would ever be right.

An hour later, Spence turned up in Derrick's office. He'd gotten back to his desk after the run-in with Abby and another half hour walking around the building, trying to make sense of the conflicting messages bombarding his brain, and saw the note. A summons of sorts.

Derrick started talking the minute Spence crossed the threshold to his plush corner office. "We have a problem."

"Our father plans on visiting, so we have more than one." Spence still hadn't figured out how he was going to handle seeing him. They hadn't spoken since the infamous kiss that ruined everything. Eldrick had tried in his usual smart-ass bragging way. Spence had ignored him and his envelope.

Derrick looked up as he settled back in his chair. "For once I'm not talking about him. I'm talking about you."

Spence stopped in midstep across the room. "Excuse me?"

"There's been a lot of talk in the office. Gossip."

There always was. That was the nature of an office. People locked into a confined space all day. They were bound to get bored and start talking about nonwork things. Spence was sure Derrick hated that reality, but it was a fact. "Since when do you care about that?"

"People have noticed the tension between you and Abby. It's been weeks and it's not getting better."

Spence felt something twist inside him. He made it to the chair across from Derrick but didn't sit in in. He stood, gripping the back with a white-knuckled grip.

"What people?" Because Spence couldn't tolerate people whispering about Abby. No matter what had happened between them now or back then, she was great at her job. She deserved the office's respect. It was not as if the past was anyone else's business anyway.

"People who work in this building. People with eyes."

"Come on." Spence refused to believe it was that widespread. He hadn't even been home a month and except for the glass-walled office kiss, he'd been careful.

"You really don't have any idea, do you?" Derrick rocked back and forth in his chair. "Well, the people who work here need to think that management is at least somewhat competent."

Fair enough. "Isn't it your job to install that faith?"

"When I'm not here, it's yours." Derrick leaned forward with his elbows balanced on the edge of his desk. "Which brings me to my point."

Spence knew they'd get there eventually. "Feel free to skip any part of this lecture."

"You need to get yourself in line." Derrick dropped that bomb then stopped talking.

Figured, his brother picked now as the perfect time to get cryptic. Spence had that sort of luck. "That's it?"

"Yes."

"Your pep talks suck, Derrick."

Light streamed in the window. Before Ellie, Derrick kept the blinds closed. Not anymore. That realization made Spence smile when nothing else about this talk did.

"You have a thing for Abby. That's not new. It's not a great idea in an office environment either, but with consent, open communication and ground rules it's workable." Derrick exhaled. "That's direct from Human Resources, by the way. I needed to be able to sleep, so I checked."

"This is about you now?"

"The point is you're avoiding how you feel about her." When Spence started to respond, Derrick talked right over him. "Unfortunately, that's not new, either. But the mess is making people twitchy, so fix it."

Spence's fingers tightened on the back of the chair. "Is this some new Human Resources program I don't know about? A sort of tough love thing?"

"The engagement party is back on. Business associates will be there. People from the office will be there. And Abby will be there." Derrick looked less happy the longer he talked.

Spence heard about the party from Ellie, so this wasn't exactly news. "Okay."

"Inside and outside of the office, you need to either deal with the fact you have feelings for Abby or bury them deep enough that they're no longer an issue."

Burying them. He'd give anything to be able to do that. "We're trying."

Derrick shrugged. "I have no idea what that means."

That made two of them. "To get along. We're trying."

Derrick laughed then. "How's that going for you?"

"It's a work in progress."

Abby sat at her desk. She'd finally stopped shaking. Spence did that to her. Got her churned up then broke her down. She didn't know how much more she could take.

With her door closed for a bit of privacy, she leaned back in the leather chair. Spun it around until she faced the windows. She looked out over the traffic. Watched a car weave in and out, riding right up on the bumpers of the ones in front of it. Talk about anxiety. It was enough to make her happy she took the metro or walked to most places.

After a few minutes, she spun her chair again. Looking at the files and the light flashing on her desk phone signaling messages, she thought about those brownies she got for Ellie. Those sounded good right now. Always, actually.

Her gaze fell on the school project file and a memory tugged at her. It took a few seconds, and then she remembered the envelope from Rylan. She reached into the folder and grabbed it. Tore the closed tab. The whole time she hoped this was work-related and not some sort of weird date invitation.

She slipped her fingers inside and took out the white piece of paper. The stationery made her heart stop. Her involuntary gasp filled the room. Berger & Associates. She knew the name all too well. Jameson's direct competition on most prestigious commercial build-out jobs.

They'd once made her a job offer. Very lucrative. All she had to do was sell her soul and spill all the proprietary information she knew about Jameson's financial dealings. Things that would give Berger the edge in bidding on jobs. Never mind that telling those secrets would likely get her sued by Derrick and make her an outcast in the DC business community.

But the timing had been interesting. Berger swooped in right after the kiss with Eldrick happened. It was as if they'd sensed her rage and vulnerability and pounced. Still, she turned them down. Angry or not, she would always turn that kind of offer down.

They'd tried a few times since but never with much enthusiasm. A call here. A stray comment at this meeting over there. Now this.

She scanned the note. It was terse and unsigned.

Basically just a date and time for a meeting and the name of a restaurant in Foggy Bottom. Then there was the last line: "You don't have a choice. Make this happen."

For the fifth time today, she got dizzy and the world flipped upside down on her. The game never ended...no matter how tired she was of playing it.

Six

The next two weeks passed in a blur. The office was on fire with work and party details. Derrick came in and out, looking and sounding grumpy and tired. The only thing that made him smile were the calls from Ellie. Spence seriously considered setting up a video system where Derrick could watch Ellie all day and maybe relax a little. Jackson told him no because he was pretty sure that crossed a line.

But Ellie had come through the weeks with little pain and no bleeding. The pregnancy was still considered high-risk and would be until the end, but Ellie had just moved into week ten and found some comfort in that, even though twelve seemed to be some sort of magic number for her.

Derrick hadn't found any peace. Spence was

pretty sure Derrick would never be calm and not panic where Ellie was concerned.

At least the party had started. Spence looked over the green lawn that stretched out behind the family's Virginia estate. Set in the country, it consisted of acres of rolling hills outlined by tall trees for privacy. A rectangular pool that no one had been in for years lay perpendicular to the house. The pristine water glistened, as did the intricate inlay of stone surrounding it.

He grew up here but hadn't been back for more than a year. Walking inside required that he exorcise more than one ghost, so he stayed outside.

His father hated anyone stepping on the lawn. The house rules were pretty strict. No one in his locked office. No one could eat dinner until he did. No noise in the house once he got home. Feet off the furniture. No running in the house. And those were the easy ones. He could go on for hours about how his property must be respected.

With that history, Spence couldn't help but smile when he saw how Derrick had set up tall tables in the grass and all along the brick pathways that led from the house to the pool, then branched off to the pool house and over to the guesthouse. People mingled and servers passed food and drinks. Soft music blasted from the outdoor speakers and lights that had been strewn above him twinkled even though the sun had not gone down.

The place had a festive air. For the first time, in what had to be more than a decade, laughter floated

around the property. People smiled and looked at
ease. Everyone seemed to be having fun, including
the mother- and wife-to-be who sat in her light blue
dress at a table closest to the back patio area with
Derrick hovering over her shoulder. She wore her
hair back and greeted guests. If an internet gossip
site hadn't announced her pregnancy prematurely,
people likely wouldn't guess.

Everything looked perfect. The party took place in
the backyard, which consisted of acres of rolling hills
and a perfectly manicured green lawn. From where
Spence stood in the rear of the soaring three-story
redbrick main house, he could watch people bustle in
and out of the four sets of French doors outlined by
columns, leading into what his father always called
the great room.

Ivy covered most of the first floor's exterior
walls. And there, standing on the second-floor balcony overhang above the house's back entrance stood
Abby. She wore a purple cocktail dress. Sort of a
lacy material that slipped over her impressive curves,
highlighting each one. Her brown hair down fell un-
bound and free. When she turned to point out something on the far lawn to Jameson Industries' head
of sales, the sun caught the strands, turning them a
lighter caramel color.

A second later, she leaned in and the older man
on the other side of her said something that made her
laugh. That open, genuine smile stole his breath. He
put his hand against his stomach without thinking.

Her body made him ache to settle the anger that lingered between them and move on to touching.

"Is it wrong that I want this over?" Jackson asked as he joined Spence at one of the high tables.

Spence forced his gaze off the woman who snagged every thought out of his head and onto the friend he'd missed as he traveled around, away from DC. "Not having fun?"

"Your father is coming. Carter is supposed to finally breeze into town. Derrick is a damn mess and there is no way Ellie is going to sit for her own engagement party." Jackson shrugged. "So, yeah. Everything is about normal around here."

"When you put it like that, I'm wondering why the two of us didn't go on an impromptu vacation and skip this." Spence saw a flash of purple and looked up again. Abby was talking to a business associate now. Someone Spence considered forgettable. But her? No. She stood out in any crowd.

Her memory lingered. Seeing her here, out of the office, lighter and not bogged down by their arguments or a stack of work, eased some of the tightness in his chest. She put in almost as many hours as Derrick usually did, but now she looked relaxed. Or she did until she started talking to this new guy.

"Well, you're in love and fighting it. I'm guessing that's your excuse."

Spence barely heard what Jackson said but he could tell from Jackson's amused expression that he needed to. He shook his head and focused in on the conversation in front of him. "What?"

"Unless you're okay with the idea of Abby dating…" Jackson spun around and pointed at a random blond-haired guy Spence had never seen before "…that guy. He was sniffing around her earlier."

The words came together in Spence's head and his insides froze. Heat washed through him, a kind of fighting preparation where his body switched to high alert and his brain kicked into gear.

"You seem pretty protective. Are you interested in her?" Because Spence had no idea what he would do then. He'd walked away from her and she was a grown-up. Next to his brothers, Jackson was his closest friend. They all considered him family. But damn.

"Hold up." Jackson put up a hand and looked like he was trying to swallow a smile. "Don't start swinging. I care about Abby as a friend. Only a friend."

Spence felt the tension ease out of him. "Oh, right."

"A friend who will beat you to death if you hurt her again."

Spence fumbled with his drink, almost dropping it before setting it down. "I didn't see that coming."

Jackson moved the glass out of spilling range. "You know Abby and I hang out all the time, right?"

"Well…no. You…you do?" Spence stammered his way through the response but his mind went blank. He didn't even remember Jackson and Abby talking all that much before he left town.

"That will teach you to go away and not visit."

Another apology Spence needed to make. He just wasn't sure how to admit that he had to go away because seeing her chipped away at him until he couldn't think straight. That he stayed gone until Derrick called because that's how he'd learned to deal with personal conflict: he stepped away from it.

"Ellie's brother is here. He seems to be behaving," Jackson said as he gestured toward a nearby table.

Noah had a history of issues, just two of which centered on decision-making and controlling his anger. He had been a huge issue in Derrick and Ellie's relationship at the start. But the twenty-year-old was brilliant and Derrick had become a mentor to him. Things were smoothing out on that front. "He's doing better. Fitting in at work and is opening up a bit to Derrick, which is kind of funny to watch."

Jackson nodded. "I love sitting in on meetings between the two of them, even though I rarely understand what Noah is saying."

Spence cleared his throat as he searched for the right words. "About me leaving—"

"She's been nervous lately, and that's not her style. I'm not sure if it's because of you or—"

"Wait a second." The conversation kept rolling and Spence had yet to catch up, but he couldn't let this part pass. "I have no intention of hurting her."

Jackson lifted his glass and took another sip. "Because you love her."

The words skidded across Spence's brain. He wanted to deny but that's not what came out. "Stop saying that."

Jackson slowly lowered his glass again. "I notice

you haven't told me I'm wrong about the love thing. Not even a 'get out of here.'"

"And I notice you waited to ambush me with this topic at a very public event."

Jackson took a sip of his beer. "I'm a pretty smart guy."

"You are." Carter stepped up to the table out of nowhere. "And trouble. Six-foot-something of pure trouble."

Seeing his baby brother, hearing that familiar amused voice, stunned Spence for a second. Carter looked the same except for the short scruff of a beard. He'd always possessed the clean-shaven baby face look. Not now. The straight black hair and black eyes were the same. He loomed tall and strong. None of that had changed.

"Carter," Spence greeted his brother then stepped back for Jackson to take a turn.

More than one head turned as the three men shook hands and hugged. Spence saw a few people point. He glanced up to the second-story deck and saw Abby watching rather than paying attention to the man talking to her.

"Who takes more than four weeks to drive across the country? How lazy are you?" Jackson asked as he flagged down a server and grabbed a glass of water for Carter.

He downed it in one sip. "I was hoping Dad would come and go before I got here."

Jackson shook his head. "You're not that lucky."

"None of us are," Spence said.

Carter reached for another glass of water from a passing tray and scanned the area. "There are a lot of people here. Do we even know this many people? I sure don't like this many people."

None of them were that great with crowds, but Carter had "it"—the charm that allowed him to talk to anyone about anything for a good twenty minutes. The sunny smile and ability to chime in at the right times. After all that interested listening, he could slip away without crushing feelings.

Most people who met him described him as the kind of guy who really listened. Spence doubted that was actually true. Carter had perfected the art of faking it. A good skill to have if you wanted to survive in the Jameson family.

"Ellie insisted if this was going to be a big party, it had to include friends, family and work people." Jackson shook his head as he spoke.

"She also demanded cupcakes," Spence said.

Carter's gaze traveled over the crowd, hesitating a few times before he spied Derrick and smiled. "Where exactly is my cupcake-eating future sister-in-law? I'm dying to meet the woman who managed to tame Derrick. She's like a miracle worker."

"You'll like her." Spence did. He couldn't imagine anyone not liking her.

"She's there." Jackson pointed at the same table Ellie had been sitting at for an hour. Derrick had moved back, but not far. "The pretty brunette talking with my sister. The other woman at the table is Ellie's best friend, Vanessa."

"Who Jackson finds very attractive." Spence had heard Jackson talk about Vanessa a few times, which was a few times more than he usually spoke about any woman in his life.

He shrugged. "I do have eyes."

"Wait a second." Carter's smile widened. "Your sister is here?"

"She's off-limits to you." Jackson grumbled something about the Jameson men being nothing but trouble.

"You've been saying that for years." Carter slapped Jackson on the back and took off. "I'll be back. Try not to burn down the house while I'm gone."

Spence watched as Carter stopped in front of Ellie and Zoe, Jackson's sister. He picked Zoe up and spun her around. After some whispering with Ellie, he pulled her to her feet and hugged her, too.

Spence shook his head. "The charmer."

"In case you were wondering, I saw Abby go into the house." Jackson peered over the top of his glass at Spence. "Just helping."

"She's free to move around."

"How very open-minded of you."

"I mean…" Yes, he wanted to talk with her. Spence could at least admit that to himself. Seeing Derrick happy and Carter at home had Spence longing for something he couldn't quite name or describe. The sensation hit him in waves and each time it crashed in, her name formed in his mind. "Fine."

"That's what I thought."

Spence reached over and polished off the rest of

Jackson's drink. "You're not as smart as you think you are."

Jackson laughed. "Yes, I am."

Abby was now very clear on what the phrase "made my skin crawl" meant. Ten minutes ago, she'd turned to leave the balcony and go down and check on Ellie. Got two steps before Jeff Berger slipped in front of her. She hadn't known he was invited but she guessed she should have assumed. His company often went up against Jameson Industries on bids. Management from both companies joked about a friendly competition between the companies. She now knew that carried with it a seedy underbelly.

"It's been a long time. I've called and haven't heard back from you." Jeff swirled the liquor in his glass. "I'm beginning to think you're ignoring me."

"Weird, right?"

"Honestly, I'm not used to that type of response."

She guessed it would cause a scene if she tossed his sorry butt off the balcony of this sweet house, so she refrained. "From women?"

"From anyone."

Lovely. But she was not surprised to hear it. Jeff had *that* look. The typical DC dude-with-money-and-connections look. He was older than Derrick by about ten ears, maybe forty-five or so. He had twin boys in private school. They played lacrosse because Jeff had. They'd probably go to some Ivy League school because Jeff did. Grow up to take over Daddy's company like Jeff intended to do.

He walked around in a fog of privilege, once commenting that it was amazing how far the Jameson family had gotten, what with having a Japanese grandmother and all. As if their background should have discounted them from making money or fitting in with the old-money boys who liked to drink their lunches on Capitol Hill restaurants.

Jeff wasn't old. There was nothing infirm about him. The receding hairline did nothing to dim what Abby supposed were his objective good looks. At least that's what other people said. He did nothing for her.

He played golf and belonged to a country club because he was supposed to, but he stayed fit. Every time there was a charity run in town, he was there with his sneakers on…making sure to get his photo taken for the newspaper. He put on a hell of a show. Abby had to give him that.

She sensed he also secretly despised Derrick and his success. "I'm surprised you're here."

Jeff's phony smile faltered a bit. "Derrick and I are business acquaintances."

"Not friends."

He made an annoying tsk-tsk sound. "What does that word even mean?"

No surprise he wouldn't be familiar with the definition. She decided to cut through the garbage and get straight to the only issue between them. "Despite the covert agent thing you did with the note—and I will be talking with Rylan about that, by the way—I won't be showing up to the meeting as ordered."

"Of course you will." Jeff took another swallow as he watched the activity on the grass below. "And do you know why, Abby? Because you are a very smart woman. You also have a lot to lose."

The anxiety churning in her stomach took off now. She'd gone from wanting to see Spence and hating how much she wanted to see him, to dreading this conversation. Life kept whizzing by her and she could not grab on and slow it down.

But she wasn't about to buy into whatever nonsense Jeff had planned. "Threats?"

"Think of this more as a conversation. One that will benefit you, if you play the game right." He leaned down with his elbows on the banister and surveyed the property as if he owned it. "After all, you wouldn't want Derrick or Spence to think you betrayed them."

The word twisted in her head. Now that he'd planted it, she doubted she'd think of anything else. "I didn't."

Jeff stood up straight again and stared down at her, letting his gaze wander all over her. "You will."

The look wasn't predatory. This was a power play. Another one she'd walked into the middle of thanks to her work. "Don't even try it, Jeff."

His eyebrow lifted. "Word is Spence is sniffing around you again. You wouldn't want to mess that up."

"Go to hell!"

He winked at her. "We'll talk soon."

* * *

Spence started up the carved staircase running up the middle of the house. It rose then stopped at a landing and split with separate staircases going off to the right and left. As kids, he and his brothers would race cars down the steps, but only when his parents weren't home to yell about the game.

This time when he looked up at the landing, he saw strappy high-heel shoes and long legs. Amazing legs. Like, killer those-things-should-be-insured legs. The edge of a purple cocktail dress. A little higher as his gaze slipped over her hips then on up.

Abby.

His heart revved. He could feel his blood pressure spike. All that talk about her and love, and there she was.

She walked down the stairs, taking her time. Enticing with a slight sway of her hips. Mentally slicing his control to shreds as she took each step. She stopped on the one above him but didn't say anything.

"There you are." His gaze met hers and the picture in his head—the one of them together, him stripping that dress off her shoulders—screeched to a halt in his head.

She smiled but it didn't reach her eyes. She scanned the downstairs as if looking for someone and not wanting to see them. His dad, maybe? Whatever was happening inside her had her looking uncharacteristically shaky and unsure.

He reached out for her hand and was surprised when she grabbed on. "Hey, are you okay?"

He guided her down to the floor, hearing the click of her heels against the polished hardwood. He slipped her hand under his arm and touched her fingers. Ice-cold.

With the fake smile in place, she cleared her voice before answering. "Fine."

"That's not really believable."

She shook her head. "Spence, I can't discuss this right now."

"Okay, wait. You're obviously upset." He guided her around the banister and into a hall. It ran the length of the right side of the house.

Leaning against the wall, he tried to block their view from the people walking in and out of the house. Many stopped and stared at the artwork trailing up the staircase and the massive chandelier hanging in the center hall. Others smiled on the way to one of the house's nine bathrooms a few doors down.

A thousand thoughts streamed through his head. He blamed his father for putting her in this state. He also played a part. So did too much work. There was a lot of responsibility to go around, but he wanted to lessen the burden. "Talk to me."

"I'm on edge and…" She shook her hands in front of her, like she was trying to get the feeling back in them.

He had no idea what was going on in her head but the aching need he had for her turned into something else. "What is it? Tell me so I can help."

She looked at him then. Met his gaze straight on. "I have all of this energy bouncing around inside me. Add in alcohol and, well, it's a combination for bad decisions."

"Am I a bad decision?" He knew the answer but asked anyway.

Her gaze traveled over him. Hesitated on his mouth, then dipped lower. To the base of his throat. "The absolute worst."

That look. It was almost as if... What the hell was happening? He grabbed on to the last of his common sense. Something was wrong. She didn't seem like herself and there was no way he was going to take advantage of that. "Maybe you should go upstairs and rest and then we can—"

"Kiss me."

That fast the world flipped on him. Tension ratcheted up. Not the I'm-worried kind but the let's-get-naked type. "Excuse me?"

"Where does that door lead?" She pointed at the one over his shoulder and when he didn't answer, she reached across him and turned the knob. A quick flick of the wall switch and the oversize pantry was bathed in light. "This will work."

He was pretty sure he was having a stroke. His muscles refused to work. He couldn't form a sentence. It was a struggle just to get out her name. "Abby..."

She backed him up against the packed shelves lining the wall. Their bodies barely touched as they brushed over each other. It was enough to set off an explosion in his head. The good kind. The kind where he wanted to touch her and taste her and do everything he'd dreamed of doing with her but figured he would never get the chance.

"I'm tired of wanting you and fighting it." She grabbed the post behind his head with one hand. The other went to the top of his shirt to play with the buttons there. "I'm tired of trying to do the right thing."

Wanting you? He was half-sure he made that part up in his head. "Abby, what's going on?"

"I'm here in this beautiful place. Watching you. Seeing all these people. Thinking about my choices." She dropped her head down to rest on his chest.

Her scent wound around him. Soft hair slid over his skin. He was pretty certain she could hear his heartbeat because it hammered loud enough to fill his ears.

Knowing he could pull back if she asked him to, because that would always be the answer for him, he slipped his fingers through her soft hair. "Is this the alcohol talking?"

"I've only had one half-filled glass of Champagne."

Her voice vibrated against his chest. Warm breath skipped over his bare skin.

There was no way he was going to survive this.

His fingers continued to gently massage the back of her neck. "I don't want to take advantage of you."

Her head shot up. "You're not your father."

"What?"

"Kiss me."

Her eyes were clear and he didn't smell alcohol. But the stench of regret would be sickening and strong if he got this moment wrong. "I'm trying not to be a jerk here."

She undid his top shirt button. Then the next. "I'll sign a release if you want or go tell a witness I asked for this or—"

"Stop talking."

He left her for a second. Didn't go far. With his hands shaking, he turned the lock on the door, grateful there was one. The mumble of voices rose and fell outside the door as people walked down the hall. No one tried to come in, but there really wasn't a reason to. At least he hoped that was true.

He looked at her, studied that stunning face and saw the heat move into her eyes. Still, they had to be clear because this could go so wrong. "Be sure."

"Spence, you are never going to get a greener light."

She stood there in that sexy dress with her hands crossed over her chest. She wasn't hiding from him. No, he got the sense she was ready. Very ready.

"You'll tell me if—"

She reached out and hooked her finger through his belt loop. Pulled him close. "Green light."

Seven

Spence's mouth covered hers and the last of her doubts blinked out. Thoughts and unwanted feelings had been whirling in her head since he stepped back into town. They came together in one blinding certainty when his hands slid up her sides—she wanted this.

Those palms cupped her breasts through her dress and her skin caught fire. She waited for the material to melt away, for her knees to give out, but somehow she stayed upright and dressed.

Those amazing fingers massaged and caressed. It took all of her control not to reach behind herself for the zipper and strip the top down. Feel him skin to skin.

"Spence…" She didn't know exactly what she wanted, so she let the whispered plea sit there.

Backing her against the shelves, he trapped her between his arms. He grabbed on to the bars on either side of her head and leaned in. Rubbed his body against hers as his mouth treated her to a heart-stopping kiss. The kind that knocked common sense far into next month.

"You are so sexy." That hot mouth traveled down her neck.

A shiver raced through her. And when those lips slipped to her ear and his tongue licked along the top edge, the shiver turned to a full-body tremble. She held on to his waist to keep from falling down.

His muscles tensed under her fingers and his breathing came harder. It thudded under her fingertips as need flashed in his eyes. He didn't do anything to hide her effect on him…and she loved that.

They broke into a wild frenzy of touching and she was knocked harder into a shelf behind her. A can crashed to the floor. Then another. She kicked them out of the way and blocked every sound, including the whooshing of her heartbeat in her ears. Her focus centered on his mouth and the energy spinning around them.

Expert hands traveled over her and around to her back. The screech of her zipper rose above the other sounds a second before his palm brushed over her bare skin. Fingers slid under her bra. The cool air hit her as the front of her dress fell down. It heated again when he lifted his head and stared at her.

Fingertips skimmed over the rounded tops of her breasts. The touch was so reverent, so loving, her breath hiccupped in her throat.

"Touch me." She breathed the order against his neck. He already was but that didn't matter to her. She wanted the imprint of his fingers all over her.

That amazing mouth kissed a trail along the top lacy edge of her bra. Her head fell back as his lips went to work. His tongue licked over her nipple as one hand slipped down the front of her in a slow slide that ignited every cell.

Needing to get closer, to bring him in, she opened her legs as wide as her dress allowed. When that didn't bring her relief, she shimmied, tugging the material up to the top of her thighs.

It was all the invitation he needed. His hand tunneled under her dress to skim along the elastic band of her underwear. The tiny bikini briefs were no defense against his fingers. They pressed up and under. Then he was touching her. Swirling his finger over her.

Need walloped her. It pressed in on her from every direction. She lifted her leg and wrapped it around his thigh. The position gave him free access and he didn't hesitate. His finger slipped inside her. Pumped back and forth until her lower body matched its rhythm.

Relief at being touched gave way to a new tension. A pounding need to feel him everywhere. "Spence, now."

A warning flashed in her mind. She was on the Pill but they should take more precautions. But the minute the thought entered her mind it left again. All of those weeks of fighting amounted to foreplay. The talking, the kissing...she was wound up and burning for him.

Her throat felt scratchy and her skin hot. She couldn't move fast enough, rip the buttons on his shirt open with enough force. Once her fingers touched the firm muscles of his chest, she dragged them down.

The shelves rattled behind her as he picked her up and wrapped both legs around him, low on his hips. Her dress bunched around her waist. He tugged on her underwear. Pulled and yanked.

"Rip it." She almost yelled the order.

"I'll buy you ten pairs," he said through harsh breaths.

His hands shook as the material tore, shredded in his hand. She didn't know if he dropped it or stripped it away. Didn't really care. She was too busy craving the weight of his body. It anchored him but she wanted more.

She fumbled with his belt as tension thumped around her. She got the zipper down and shoved the material out of the way. When she wrapped her fingers around his length, he swore then took in a big gulping breath. His control seemed to snap. With jerky movements, he put a hand over hers and squeezed and the resulting groan vibrated through him.

Between his finger inside her and his mouth on her neck, her body flipped to ready. She arched her hips, trying to drag him inside her. When that failed, she slipped her thumb over his tip. His body actually fell forward. The shelves clanked behind her as they moved, but she didn't care.

They could have been screaming, drawing the attention of everyone at the party, but none of that mattered. Just the man wrapped around her and the feel of his mouth on her skin.

"Now, Spence." She was two seconds from begging.

She opened her mouth to do it when she felt him. Just the tip, rubbing over her. Back and forth, moving deeper with each pass. Then he pushed inside her. Slow, in a seduction that had her hips bucking. As he shifted, her internal muscles adjusted and clamped down on him, clinging to him.

"Damn, Abby." He was panting now as his arms supported her and his mouth traveled to that sensitive space right behind her ear.

When a noise rumbled up her chest, she put the back of her hand over her mouth and bit it. But her control faltered with each delicious thrust. The steady in and out had her body tightening. Every cell pulsed. After one last push inside her, she came apart. The orgasm screamed through her as her hips continued to move back and forth.

He kept plunging as the sweat broke out at the base of his neck. When her body started to wind down, she concentrated on him. Kissed that sexy collarbone and dragged her teeth along his neck.

That's all it took. He moaned as his hips tipped forward one last time. His fingers tightened on the back of her thighs. She held on as the orgasm hit him. His body rocked against her and she felt it all. Finally, his head dipped until his forehead rested against her chest. The pulses continued for a few more seconds before his body relaxed and his weight pressed heavier against her.

His labored breathing blew across her chest. The sleek muscles of his back tensed as she traced her fingers over them. She tried to soothe him with gentle kisses on the top of his head.

After a few seconds, he turned his head to the side and rested his cheek against her chest. "Well, that was amazing."

She had no idea where he found the energy to speak. She couldn't even manage to use that breathy voice like he did. Her muscles refused to listen as her body curled into his.

"Yeah." That took all she had but at least she managed to whisper something into his hair.

He lifted his head and stared down at her. Those sexy eyes, all intense and unreadable, watched her. "Any regrets?"

His voice sounded scratchy and oh-so-sexy. She knew she could be coy or play games, but she couldn't muster up the energy for that, either. "None."

A second later, the doorknob rattled and they both jumped. Their bodies hadn't separated or cooled. They both held their breaths. After a second shake of the knob, the voices in the hall died down and whoever was out there seemed to move away.

"That was close," she said, even though she didn't care.

She knew she should slide down, enjoy the friction until their bodies separated. She rested her head against his instead.

"Abby?"

With all the stress and worry gone, exhaustion hit her. But her eyes popped open again just as they were beginning to close. "Yeah?"

"Next time, we use a bed."

It took another fifteen minutes for them to break apart. Spence couldn't stop kissing her while they straightened their clothes and cleaned up a bit. He didn't even try to hold back. The last one came as he pulled up the zipper to her dress. Before finishing the last inch, he leaned down and pressed a kiss on the bare skin of her shoulder. Tried to remember every scent and feeling so he could relive this moment later.

When she turned around to face him, he expected regret and maybe a little shyness. Instead, she smiled up at him. "Does my hair look like we just had sex?"

Every part of her did, but he figured that had more to do with his needs and his perception than with the state of her clothes and makeup. "You look amazing."

"We need to leave this room." She sighed. "I'm sure someone has been looking for us."

Knowing his family, many *someones* were. Maneuvering through the next twenty minutes might not be that easy. It would help if he could forget that he carried her ripped panties in his pocket. "I envy you being an only child at the moment."

She smiled and opened the door. Peeked out while he stole one last look at her perfect butt. The woman filled out a slim-fitting dress better than any woman he'd ever known. She was curvy and sleek…and he would have to concentrate very hard not to think about what she could do with that mouth.

They'd just stepped into the hall when Carter appeared in front of them. That grin. The way his gaze wandered over both of them.

This was not going to be good. Spence would bet money on that.

"Where were you two?" Carter asked as he glanced into the dark pantry behind them.

Abby's eyes widened. "What?"

"Hmm?" Spence asked at the same time.

Carter's grin only grew bigger. "Was that a hard question?"

Leave it to his baby brother to pick this moment to come home after months away. Now he was showing up everywhere. The guy's timing sucked. "Of course not."

Carter gestured for them to go into the library two doors down the hall. Since complying struck Spence as the quickest way through this situation, he followed. They all stepped inside and were immediately surrounded by walls of books. A desk sat in the corner by the large floor-to-ceiling window. There were a few other chairs scattered around the room but they stood there, with the door closed behind them.

Carter looked from Abby to Spence and back again. "You missed the toast to the happy couple."

"Well…" Yeah, that's all Spence had. His brain refused to jump-start after the mind-blowing sex.

"Ellie can't drink anyway," Abby said, piping up to fill the silence.

"Yes." Spence nodded. "Good. That's right."

Carter shook his head, looking far too amused by the stilted conversation. "Because that was my point."

"We're just…" It happened again. Spence started talking, then nothing. His mind went blank.

Abby touched the back of her hand against his chest. "Walking."

"Wow." Carter crossed his arms over his chest. Looked pretty impressed with himself, as if every minute was more fun than the last. "You two aren't very good at this. Maybe you need practice."

"What are you talking about?" Abby asked.

The door opened behind them and Jackson slipped inside, sparing Spence from whatever answer Carter might have come up with to Abby's question. Jackson's shoes clicked against the buffed hardwood floor as he walked. He'd picked up a piece of cake at some point and now balanced that plate along with his glass. With his fork raised halfway to his mouth he started talking.

"I heard you guys were in here. Where did you…" His gaze switched from Abby to Spence. "Oh."

Carter snorted. "Right?"

"I give up. Are we wearing a sign?" Abby finished the question by glaring at Spence.

He wasn't sure what he did to warrant that, or maybe he did, but he knew no matter what had happened in that pantry, this embarrassment was going to be his fault. No way would Carter let this opportunity pass.

"Kind of." Carter cleared his throat as he pointed at Spence's chest. "Your shirt is—"

"Buttoned wrong, genius." Jackson shook his head as he put his drink on the edge of the desk and scooped up a forkful of cake.

After a quick look at Spence, Abby rolled her eyes. "You had one job."

A guy could not catch a break around here. Spence went to work on fixing the misbuttoning. "Excuse me, but my brain is not working at top-speed right now."

No one said anything for a few seconds. Spence knew he should jump in and clean up his last comment but what the hell did he say?

When the quiet dragged on, Carter rubbed his hands together. "So, how do you want us to handle this?"

"With a little dignity would be nice," Abby mumbled as she threw them all a men-suck glance.

"We're all grown-ups." Jackson's gaze moved around the group before landing on Spence. "For the most part."

"Right. We've all had sex. Not together, of course." Carter was just revving up, speaking faster as he went when he glanced at Abby and his words sputtered out. "What? Are we dancing around the word? At least I hope it was good sex. You were both smiling a few minutes ago."

"I can think of a thousand places I'd rather be right now," Abby said in an emotionless voice.

"So that it's official and since I know introducing myself shouldn't get me in too much trouble compared to whatever else I might say, I'm Carter Jameson." He held out his hand to Abby.

She took it as she frowned at him. "We've actually met before."

Carter's eyes narrowed. "We have?"

Spence thought back to the calls he shared with Carter all those months ago. The complaints about Dad and his behavior. Talks about the kiss and how sick he felt at seeing it. He hoped Carter forgot every last word. "Be careful."

"I'm Abby Rowe." She finished shaking his hand, then dropped her arm to her side again. "I work for your company. On the management team, actually. We used to pass in the halls. Not often but sometimes when you were in the office visiting your brothers."

"I don't… Oh." Carter's eyes widened. "Okay, yeah."

Jackson nodded. "Subtle."

"You'd be less annoying if you didn't smile so big right now." Abby shot Carter her best watch-it look as she talked.

"Sorry." Carter had the grace to wince as he looked at Abby. Then he turned to Spence. "So, is she why you came back home so fast when Derrick called for help?"

This discussion just got worse and worse. It was as

if Carter didn't have a filter. Spence wanted the talk before Abby unleashed and kicked them all. "Hey, Carter? Shut up."

The noise from the hallway grew louder right before the door pushed open. Spence's vision refused to focus...but then it did. He saw a couple—him in his sixties, tall with a regal look to him. Her in her forties with shoulder-length auburn hair and a smile that looked like it was plastered on her face against her will.

Eldrick and the newest missus. All dressed up with her in flowing off-white pants and a matching shirt, and him in navy pants and a blazer. The type of outfit that suggested he'd rather be on a boat.

The only thing that made the unwanted meeting tolerable was that Eldrick's newest wife looked even less excited to be there than any of his children. Spence almost felt sorry for her. Officially meeting the family for the first time like this couldn't be easy. Especially *this* family.

"I see your behavior has not improved since we last saw each other, Spencer." That familiar stern Dad voice floated through the room.

All of the amusement drained from Carter's face. "Dad."

"When did you get here?" Spence didn't mean for it to come out like an accusation but even he heard the edge to his tone.

"I just arrived. You remember Beth." Eldrick gestured toward his wife.

For a second, Spence thought he missed a marriage. They'd eloped and Derrick and Spence had only seen her once, even then only briefly and as she stepped on a private plane at the airport. Carter never had. But that wasn't the name Spence remembered. "I thought your name was Jackie."

She nodded. "Jacqueline Annabeth Winslow Jameson."

That was quite something. Spence felt a headache coming on.

"She prefers…" Eldrick smiled as he looked around the room, and then his mouth fell into a flat line. "Abigail."

Without a word, Abby picked up Jackson's glass and threw the contents in Eldrick's face. They all jumped back, and Beth or Jackie or whatever her name was this week gasped.

Abby didn't even blink. "Welcome home."

Eight

Abby's brain had clicked off. Just seeing Eldrick pushed her into a killing rage. He stood there, smiling while he acted as if everyone around him should jump to his command. When he said her name, her brain snapped. All those months of seething backed up on her and she grabbed the drink. Not her usual move but she refused to regret it.

She'd heard people whisper about his good looks. They hadn't faded as he'd aged. He still possessed that country-club air. The salt-and-pepper hair matched his trim frame. The Champagne dripping down his shirt and stuck in tiny droplets in his hair, not so much.

She hated every inch of his smug face.

She looked around the room. No one seemed

angry, but Eldrick sputtered as he wiped his hands down his shirt. His wife patted her hand against his chest, as if that would somehow dry the material.

Well, they could all stare at her or be furious—even kick her out—Abby didn't care. Eldrick deserved to be drenched. That and so much more.

"What in the world was that about?" Jackie-Now-Beth asked.

"Ask him." Because Abby wanted to see if he would say it to her face. Spew his lies with her standing right there, ready to pounce.

"Okay." Jackson put out both hands as if trying to calm down the room. "Let's all relax for a second."

"Jackson is right. Let's not get excited. It isn't as if that's the first time someone doused Dad in a drink in this house." Carter shook his head. "I can think of at least two other wives who used that trick."

Abby liked him.

"Carter, not now." Spence issued the order without moving his gaze from her.

He still didn't get it. That realization moved through Abby, nailing her to the floor. After the sex and the flirting, even the fighting, he didn't see the truth. He still believed she was a willing participant in that kiss with his father back then.

Some of the fight ran out of her at the thought but she would not back down. Eldrick could not weasel out of this confrontation by throwing his weight around or running away to get married. She stood right in front of him because he needed to face her. He owed her this moment.

"That was unnecessary." Eldrick kept his voice even as he threw a scowl in Abby's general direction.

That ticked her off even more. "You made my life miserable."

"Who are you?" Beth asked. There wasn't any heat in her voice. More like a mix of confusion and concern.

Abby didn't know what to think about Beth. In her shoes, if she were married and in love, she'd go ballistic if someone attacked her husband. Then in private, she would shake him until he told her the truth.

But she asked, so… "I'm Abby. I work at Jameson Industries and—"

"Not if you keep behaving like that." The anger edged Eldrick's tone now. The threat hovered right there but he didn't drop it. "Do you understand me?"

He talked to her like she was a child. Dismissive. The man was completely annoying. She had no idea how he'd produced or had any part in raising his otherwise decent sons.

"No one is firing her." Spence's tone was clear and firm. The underlying beat of don't-test-me rang in his voice.

Abby couldn't figure out if that was aimed at her or his father…or both. She tried to ignore the part of her that cared what he thought. She had to block every memory of his touch and the way his mouth felt against her skin to get through this. Fury fueled her now and she couldn't back down. She needed all of her focus now. She'd waited for so long for this moment. It was happening.

She turned to Beth, not sure if the woman was an ally or not. "Your husband, on those occasions when he bothered to come into the office, would corner me. He talked about how we should have private dinners. Commented on my skirt length."

Carter's mouth dropped open. "What?"

"When was this?" Beth asked as she shifted a bit. One minute she was tight up against her husband's side. The next she put a bit of space between them.

Abby had expected the other woman to lash out and aim all of her disbelief right at Abby, not believing any accusations. But Beth looked engaged. Maybe she'd always suspected her husband could cross the line. Abby wasn't sure. Beth's eyes had narrowed but she wasn't yelling or shouting about Eldrick's imaginary good points.

That was enough to encourage Abby to keep going. "It happened right up until the time he left to marry you."

"That's not true." Eldrick took a step in Abby's direction. "You stop this."

Spence blocked his path. "Let her talk."

That's exactly what she intended to do, with or without their permission. She'd laid this out for Human Resources at the office right after it happened. They'd called Derrick in and then she'd shut down. She knew she needed to own that piece, but back then the idea of going up against a wall of Jamesons had panicked her. She needed to hold on to her job, at least until she'd found something else.

It took her months to realize Derrick wasn't his

father. Derrick would have believed her, but by then the damage had been done and Spencer was gone. She'd lost all she could tolerate losing and Eldrick was no longer around to cause trouble, so she let the complaint drop. But now he was back, and that meant he was fair game. She refused to let anyone else suffer because of him.

Which mentally brought her to the hardest part of her story. The part she once tried to tell Spence but he was too busy storming off to listen. "You kissed me. Grabbed me in my office and told me that Spence was wrong for me."

Carter moved then. He turned to face his father. "You did what?"

She couldn't stop now. The words spilled out of her. "He bragged about how Spence would never believe me. How he'd see us together and immediately blame me and bolt."

"Oh, man. That's messed up."

She was pretty sure that comment came from Jackson. She didn't look around to see, but Carter and Spence seemed frozen. Neither of them moved. The only sign of life she could pick up in Spence was the way his hands balled into fists at his sides.

"Okay, look." Eldrick held up his hand as he stepped into the center of the group. "You're exaggerating this a bit, don't you think?"

She refused to stop now or let this slide. This time he needed to face the consequences, even if they only amounted to her yelling at him. "You thought it was funny to see Spence back down."

When Eldrick took another step, Spence grabbed his arm and pulled him back. "Funny? How could you possibly think that?"

"I was saving you, as usual."

Spence made a choking sound. "You can't be serious."

"She worked for you. It was too risky for you to make a move. I was proving a point. It all worked out." Eldrick had the nerve to shake his head.

Between what he said and the patronizing tone in which he said it, Abby wanted to punch him. Worse, open that door and yell her accusations into the hall so that everyone in that big house, on that massive property, knew the kind of man Eldrick really was.

Eldrick stared down at Spence's hand on his arm. "It was a matter of containing the potential damage. We both know you weren't in it for the long term, so why endanger our position? Dating was too risky. The potential liability outweighed whatever feelings you thought you had."

Before Abby could say anything else, Beth turned to her husband. "Eldrick?"

Abby couldn't read the other woman. She stood tall and her voice never wavered. Abby knew almost nothing about her. No one at work talked about her. Jackson had said something about her being different from the other wives. Not as young. Not demanding or the type to run through money, except for her request that they move away and enjoy life on the beach.

One look from his wife and Eldrick's stern I'm-in-charge-here glare faltered. His tone morphed into a lighter, more cajoling sound. "Beth, it's not—"

"We were engaged when this happened. You hadn't announced it to your family, but you had asked. I wore the ring."

Eldrick shot a look in Abby's direction. She sensed a hint of desperation. He no longer stood there as if he could kick them all out at any minute, even though he likely could.

Good, let him squirm.

He shrugged. "Help me out here."

"You've got to be kidding." Abby crossed her arms in front of her to telegraph the very simple message that the man was on his own.

"She could have sued you." Beth took a step closer to Abby. "It sounds like she should have. And hurting your own son? Your behavior was appalling."

The move was so sudden that Abby lost her balance. She leaned against Beth for a second before straightening up again.

"I figured he was protected. It's his company, after all," Abby explained.

An odd sound escaped Spence. "Abby, you can't believe that his behavior would have been okay with us. With me."

She almost said words that would cut him down. The sentence was right there. *You were too busy running away to care.* The only thing that stopped her was Spence's pained expression. "He was in charge, Spence. He'd *been* in charge, had that big corner office that Derrick now uses. I didn't know how many other women—"

"None." Eldrick practically yelled the response.

Carter snorted. "That's doubtful."

Abby blew out a long breath and spilled the last of the truth as she looked at Spence. "I didn't know who to trust."

The hit didn't land any lighter because of her softer tone. She saw Spence wince. So did Jackson. But she wasn't aiming at either of them. Her target, the man she ached to hurt, stood right in front of her.

In the last few seconds he seemed to have lost some of his height. His shoulders fell and he stared at his wife as if he wasn't sure how to approach her.

"Beth, listen to me." Eldrick's hand brushed against Beth's arm.

"Did you really say those things to Abby?" When he didn't immediately answer her, Beth's eyebrow arched. "Well?"

She sounded like a mom now. A really ticked off one. Abby remembered that you're-in-trouble tone from her childhood.

Finally, Eldrick exhaled. "I don't remember exactly what I said."

Relief soared through Abby. Some of the tension eased from her body, leaving her feeling lighter. "Which means yes."

Eldrick snapped at her. "This isn't your business."

"How can you say that?" Carter asked in a voice that still sounded stunned and confused. "This is about her."

"And Spence is your son, Eldrick." Beth shook her head before glancing over at Abby. "Were you and Spence actually dating back then?"

Before she could answer, Spence jumped in. "We were starting to. I was hopeful."

Those words… Abby never expected to hear him admit that out loud, because that moment had passed. She'd spent so much time being angry and hurt because he didn't believe her. Because he didn't stick around long enough to listen to her. She'd never stopped to think about what he saw. That didn't forgive any of his behavior, but it meant something to see how broken he looked and sounded now that he knew the truth.

He did care.

Beth turned back to her husband. "What is wrong with you?"

"I've been asking that for years," Carter said half under his breath.

Eldrick shot Carter a withering look before answering. "Beth, this is a family matter."

"I am your wife now."

For once, Abby thought that was a good thing. This woman did not back down or buy into Eldrick's ramblings. But she clearly deserved a better husband.

After a few seconds, Eldrick seemed to mentally calm down. His shoulders relaxed and the ruddy color on his cheeks vanished. "We should talk in private."

Beth nodded. "Let's go."

"I haven't seen Derrick and his fiancée yet." One look at Beth's face and Eldrick nodded. "Fine."

Without another word, they walked across the library and opened the door. Eldrick didn't look back or say anything as they stepped into the hallway and closed the door behind them.

Abby didn't realize she'd been holding her breath until it seeped out of her. She suddenly felt dizzy and her throat ached. She'd been feeling off for a few days but chalked that up to all the energy she was using trying to tamp down on her attraction to Spence. Now she figured the draining fatigue came from finally letting all of her frustration out.

Carter smiled at her in a way that looked almost like an apology. "Happy?"

"I'm not unhappy." Tired and out of words, yes.

Spence stepped in front of her then. His face was pale and the sexy grin from the pantry was long gone. "Abby."

He probably wanted to talk it out, but she couldn't do it. She needed a break. A few minutes of quiet. "I want to go home."

He nodded as his voice stammered. "Of course. I'll take you."

"No, I will." Jackson backed Spence away. "You Jamesons probably need to talk this out."

"I don't—"

"Hey." Carter caught Spence's arm and pulled him back. "Give her a minute, Spence."

She appreciated the support. With her head spinning and her knees weak, she doubted she could get out of there without falling down. She'd never appreciated Jackson's supportive arm as much.

But a part of her did ache for Spence. For the grief and pain she saw in his eyes. For the way his mouth dropped open and stayed there, as if he didn't know what to say.

She tried to smile at him but couldn't quite get there. "We'll talk soon."

She gave his arm a quick squeeze, and then she was gone.

Spence couldn't move. His brain screamed to go after her. Forget Carter's well-meaning warnings and Jackson's small head shake. He'd screwed this up in every way possible. Let his history with his father ruin his chance with Abby.

Back then it had seemed so simple. His father made moves on women all the time. Married or not, he was always looking for what else was out there. He'd flirted with women Spence dated until he learned never to bring them around the house or work. Having a thing for Abby, who was right there in the office, threw Spence's usual routine out of whack. He couldn't keep her away from his dad.

That was his one defense. He'd been using it since high school when Spence walked into the kitchen one night and saw his dad standing at the sink with his hand on Spence's then-girlfriend's lower back. They were whispering and laughing. He doubted anything actually happened, but it was so wrong. Dominating and sick.

Spence had been wary and on the lookout ever since. So, when he walked in on that kiss he thought… Bile rushed up the back of his throat at the memory.

"What is going on?" Derrick burst into the library, frowning and wide-eyed with confusion. "You all disappeared and Abby just ran out of here. Not actually, but she sure looked spooked."

Carter frowned. "Dad."

"Eldrick is here?" Derrick's mouth fell and his tone flattened. "Lucky us."

"He and Beth—"

"Wait." Derrick held up a hand. "Who is Beth?"

"Yeah, that's a confusing piece of the story. Apparently, we call his wife Beth now. Believe it or not, you'll like her." Carter shook his head. "But the point is Dad admitted to sexually harassing Abby and setting her up with that kiss to scare Spence off."

Spence appreciated Carter's explanation because he wasn't sure he could get one out right now. He wasn't sure of anything. He glanced at his watch, trying to calculate how much time he should wait before going to see Abby. Jackson might have the answer. Spence half hoped Jackson also would know what to say because Spence was clueless. There wasn't an apology big enough to handle this.

"I can't…" Derrick slipped his fingers through his hair. "I asked her back then, but…" He looked at Carter. "Is she okay?"

Carter shrugged. "She unloaded, so hopefully she will be."

"What about you?" Derrick glanced at Spence. "You okay?"

"No."

Carter gave him a reassuring pat on the shoulder. "You will be, too. Give it time."

Spence wasn't convinced.

Nine

Spence waited for two days. Sunday dragged by with him texting Abby and not receiving a response. Carter had convinced him to wait a little longer and Ellie agreed. Jackson fed him some updates. On Monday, she didn't show up for work and Spence's nerves were shot. He had this image of her packing and leaving town. That was his thing and he was desperate for her not to repeat his mistakes.

The sick thing sounded like subterfuge. Derrick said that never happened. He couldn't remember a day Abby had missed since starting with the company. And that did it. Spence spent the afternoon trying to come up with a plan that didn't come off controlling and rude like his father. Spence didn't want to be that guy. Ever.

But she was in hiding. Not her style and not something Spence had expected, but that's what he got. He had to deal with it. True, she deserved some peace and time to think. He tried to give it to her. He really did. But at seven on Monday night, he stepped into the lobby of her condo building and met up with Jackson.

"I hope I don't regret letting you in," Jackson said as they walked to the elevator.

Yeah, that made two of them. "Get in line."

The fact Jackson was comfortable there, that he got in and out and on the security-protected elevator without trouble had Spence's mind spinning. He grabbed on to the bar behind him in the elevator as the car started to move. He hoped the stranglehold would keep him from doing or saying something stupid.

After a few seconds of silence, he opened his mouth anyway. "She's—"

"Not expecting you," Jackson said.

Spence couldn't figure out if that was a good idea or not. Showing up unannounced might be a jerk move. Honestly, he'd pulled so many with her he couldn't tell where the line was anymore.

"Are you planning to stick around and referee?" Part of Spence didn't hate the idea. Strength in numbers and all that. Having reinforcements might not be bad, either, since he expected Abby to be furious.

The rest of him wanted Jackson out. The majority part. This was private, or it should be. The unloading, the telling of what happened back then, played out in front of an audience. She deserved an empty room for whatever else she needed to say. And he would take it. He owed her that much.

"You really have been gone a long time." A mass of keys and security fobs jangled in Jackson's hand.

"What?"

Jackson shook his head as he smiled. "I forgot we've been hanging out over at Derrick's place or going out to eat since you've been back. So, you don't know."

The elevator bell dinged and the doors opened. Spence stepped out into the hall, not sure where to go or how to interpret Jackson's unusual ramblings.

"Any chance you're going to explain?" Spence asked.

Jackson nodded. "Follow me."

He turned left and started down the hall. Stopped in front of the first door and pointed at it. "She lives here."

Then he kept walking. Got to the next door and stopped. "This is mine."

Spence's heart stopped. For a second, he couldn't breathe. "You live in the same building? On the same floor?"

Next to each other. That struck Spence as convenient and frustrating, and his anxiety spun out of control inside him.

"Abby told me about a good deal. I jumped in, bought low and became her neighbor." Jackson winked at him. "But before you panic, and I can see it welling up in you already, I'm still only her good friend. Nothing more."

"Why?" Spence couldn't imagine another man not wanting her. Not making a move. Loyalty, sure, and none of the brothers or Jackson had ever tried to ask another's ex out, but still. The proximity, their clear chemistry.

"It was never going to happen." Jackson shook his head. "Because you love her."

There was that word again. Spence kept waiting for his brain to reject it, but it didn't happen.

The lock clicked and Jackson opened his door. "Don't mess this up."

When the bell bonged, Abby glared at the front door to her condo. She'd just sank down into the corner seat of her sectional. Arranged the blankets and pillows just right around her. Had a box of tissues on one side. The remote control on her lap. Medicine, water bottle and a cup of lemon tea right in front of her.

When the bell rang out a second time, she cursed under her breath. This could only be a handful of people. No one buzzed to come upstairs. The phone didn't ring from the front desk to ask her permission to send someone to her. Jackson had a key. That left someone in the building or maintenance.

She stomped across her living room, ignoring the way her bright purple slippers clapped against the hardwood floor. She wore sweatpants and a shirt. No bra. Someone was about to get a show.

She peeked in the peephole and froze. Clearly the bad cold or the medicine or just life in general was making her vision blur. There was no way Spence stood out there. None.

"What?" She shouted the question through the door.

"Abby, please let me in."

Yep, same silky voice. A defeated muffled tone, maybe, but that probably had something to do with him standing in the hallway.

But there was no use in ignoring him. That was easy on the phone. Harder when he hovered outside her door. She opened it and stared at him. "What?"

Whatever tough stance she was trying to take likely was ruined when she sniffled. Stupid cold.

He frowned at her. "You really are sick?"

Of all the things he could have said, that one was unexpected. "Of course. I don't hide. Like I'd give your father that satisfaction."

Oh, she'd wanted to. She'd even toyed with the idea. When the fever hit her on Saturday night after the big showdown with Eldrick, she'd chalked it up to frazzled nerves. By the next morning when she couldn't lift her head off the pillow, she realized it was something else.

Needing to sit down, she left Spence at the door and walked back to her sectional. The cushions had never looked so inviting. She flipped off the slippers and slid into her cocoon of covers. Didn't even look at him again until her head rested against the pillows propping her up from behind.

He stood over her, watching her. His gaze traveled over her. Not sexual. No, this felt like he was conducting an inventory. "When did you get sick?"

"I'd been fighting it off for about a week." She lifted her head in the direction of the pill bottle on the ottoman. "I took some medicine I happened to have here and thought I caught it in time, but no."

He sat on the edge of the couch. About a foot away from her. "It's not healthy to self-medicate."

"You sound like my doctor." She was kind of tired of men telling her she was wrong about things. Not a rational response, she knew. But still.

He looked around the condo. His gaze zipped to her modern kitchen and the sleek white quartz countertop. To the dishes piled in her sink. "Have you eaten?"

She cuddled deeper into the cushions and let his deep voice wash over her. "It's amazing what you can have delivered in this town."

"True."

That's all he said. He didn't move or try to get closer. She sensed he wanted to say something and she was not in the mood to make any of this easier on him. Now wasn't the right time and she didn't have the strength to carry on much of a conversation, but she could sit there and listen.

"I'll handle these." He stood up and stripped off his suit jacket. Threw it over her chair. The stupid thing hung there like it belonged in her condo.

She hated that.

"What are you talking about?" she asked as she watched those long legs carry him to the other side of the condo.

He stepped into the open kitchen and rolled up his shirtsleeves. "The dishes."

Did he just say… "Are you kidding?"

He shrugged. "Seems like the least I can do."

"You know how to do dishes?"

He looked up at her. "I'm not totally useless."

"No one said *totally*."

She thought she saw him smile at her joke as he went to work. Those long fingers soaped up the dishes. She considered reminding him she had a dishwasher, but it was right there. Surely he could see it.

No, she sensed this was something else. As if he were paying penance.

He cleaned in silence for the first five minutes. Then he started to talk. "I learned young to shut down. My dad would yell because nothing was ever good enough for him. I'd take myself out of the middle of it. Some days, he and Derrick would go at it." Spence shook his head as if he were reliving a memory in his mind. "Unbelievable."

She didn't say anything. The cadence of his voice comforted her. Getting a peek into his childhood seemed to chase some of the germs away.

"Eldrick Jameson is not a good man. He was a terrible, distant, mean father. Hell, he wasn't even much of a businessman. Derrick had to rescue the company from Dad's overspending and bad choices." Spence folded the towel and hung it on the bar on the stove. "Other kids had it much worse. I get that. We never wanted for anything. Dad kept up the outside appearances. Played the role of family man."

Abby thought about Eldrick's series of marriages. Of all the goodwill he'd run through in his life.

Spence walked back into the living room. She moved over a bit to silently tell him he could sit next to her.

He took the hint. Dropped into the cushions and snaked his arm along the back of the sectional. Didn't touch her. Didn't even come close, but having him near felt reassuring in an odd way.

"You weren't the first girlfriend he approached… and I know I'm taking liberties with that word." He waited until she nodded to continue. "But he'd made passes before. Sometimes the ploy worked, sometimes not. It chipped away at my trust of him and the women I was attracted to. Of myself."

Spence picked at a spot on the cushion. Sat in silence for a few seconds before continuing. "He knew I was likely to run if he pushed too hard and tested me all the time. Made it clear I didn't deserve anything in the company or in the way of a home life because I hadn't proven myself."

"He really was terrible." She hadn't meant to say that. It slipped out but it wasn't wrong.

"Still is, though Beth might turn out to be one of his better choices." Spence exhaled. "He's currently sending us through this list of tasks we have to perform in order for him to turn the company over."

"What's yours?"

"I don't know." Spence barked out a harsh laugh. "He gave Derrick an envelope for me but I never opened it. I was too busy trying to figure out where we stood."

We? She had no idea but she wasn't ready for this conversation either. "Spence, I—"

"I'm not asking. It was just an explanation." His hand dropped and his fingers moved closer to her shoulder, but he still didn't touch her.

She sensed he might not unless she gave permission. And that was not going to happen…yet.

"I learned this defense. Carter and I both did. We took off. Carter traveled. I tried to forget everything here and all my regrets."

She tipped her head back and looked at him. Let her gaze linger over his tired face and the dark circles under his eyes. "Am I a regret?"

"You are amazing. Smart and beautiful, funny and quick." He shot her a cute smile. "Sexy as hell. That pantry was basically every one of my fantasies brought to life." His smile faded. "But I messed up before. I do regret running out on you, not believing you. Breaking your trust before I really had a chance to earn it."

"I guess you had a reason not to trust so easily." She'd never admitted that before. Never even let it enter her head. In every scenario that ran through her mind, she was the sole victim in Eldrick's schemes. But now she saw that wasn't quite true.

"Don't give me an out, Abby." His fingers slipped lower then. Right next to her shoulder. Brushing against it in a soothing gesture. "I'm a grown man.

I was done playing Eldrick's games but that doesn't excuse leaving you here to deal with him."

"He bolted soon after." She had been so happy that day. Happy every day since when he stayed gone.

Spence shook his head. "That's not my point."

She lifted her hand and covered his. Let their fingers tangle together. "I know."

They sat there in silence. Images ran across the television screen. She'd turned the sound off when the doorbell rang and hadn't turned it back on. Now they both watched the show, some detective thing with a lot of running, without any noise or talking.

She tugged him a bit closer. Felt the cushion dip when he slid over and wrapped an arm around her shoulders. The sex had been so good. Not smart, because she hadn't insisted on a condom and at some point they needed to talk about that, but hot and right and almost cleansing in the force of it. But this felt pretty great, too. The silence. The calm.

Her fingers slipped over the remote, but she still didn't turn on the sound. She didn't want to break the mood. Not when she could concentrate on the way his breath blew over her forehead, and how every now and then, he would turn his head to place a chaste kiss on her hair.

"I know I need to earn back your trust," he said into the quiet as darkness fell outside the windows behind the couch. "I just want you to think about giving me the chance to do that."

Hope soared inside her and her heartbeat kicked up. The traitorous thing. The answer *yes* screamed inside her head but she didn't say it out loud. Not yet. Not when Eldrick was still in town and Spence's propensity to flee hadn't been resolved. And she still needed to deal with Jeff Berger and whatever stupid thing he had planned for her.

She glanced up at Spence. Let her gaze wander over his lips. "I actually am hungry."

A smile broke out on his lips. This one genuine and warming. "What do you want?"

She turned just a bit under his arm so she could see him better. "You mean you can cook, too?"

"I order things." He suddenly looked so serious. "I'm really good at ordering."

The joking almost did her in, but she held on to her control. This would take time to fix. "You just ruined my image of you as this big domestic guy who could do anything in the house."

His eyebrow lifted. "Oh, I have skills. When you're feeling better, I'll show you."

Her heart jumped. "Interesting." Man, it so was.

"But for now…" He lifted his hips and slid his phone out of his back pocket. Started clicking on the keys. "You're getting soup."

It was the right answer but she wrinkled up her nose at the suggestion anyway. "I want a burger."

He shot her a side-eye. "I'll buy you as many as you want as soon as you're feeling better."

"That's a pretty good incentive to get well." So was he, but she didn't mention it.

"Then soup it is." He dropped a quick kiss on

her forehead. "We'll get back to the good stuff soon enough."

For the first time in months she believed that. "You're on."

Ten

The next week passed by in a happy blur. They didn't get naked again, which Spence regretted, but it was the right answer. He was willing to give Abby as much time as she needed and hoped the answer wasn't forever.

She was feeling better and back to work, having missed only one day. Her so-called easier schedule quickly gave way to long meetings and even longer workdays. They went to dinner, talked, watched movies on her sectional, and then he went home each night after a lingering kiss. That was the new cycle.

Since Beth had dragged Eldrick right back out of town after the scene in the Virginia estate library, it was easy to ignore his calls. Even easier to ignore the stupid envelope with his To Do list for keeping the business. It sat unopened on the dresser in the bedroom Spence still used in Derrick and Ellie's house. She was still resting but up more. Keeping Carter entertained and Derrick smiling.

It was all so normal. Well, normal for other people. Spence didn't know what to do or what to think. He stayed on edge, waiting for the bad news to come. Because it always did.

In her second week back, they had a morning status meeting, covering several projects, and then Abby had a business lunch. Something she'd been putting off and moved on her calendar twice. He didn't know what it was but he trusted her. They were...*dating*. He guessed that was the right word, but who knew. He wasn't about to ask, because he didn't want to scare her away. Not when things were going well.

Right now she was sitting in a conference room chair, pummeling Rylan with questions. "When will the report be done?"

He shifted the papers around in front of him on the conference room table. Abby had insisted on scheduling them for the big room. The one with expensive artwork hanging on the walls and the blackout curtains. It spoke to the company's success and provided a level of intimidation.

The whole thing was wildly enjoyable for Spence to watch.

"I need—"

"Rylan, I am done playing with this." Abby leaned back in her chair. "You know I am."

Something had changed in the relationship between Abby and Rylan. It had always been professional, respectful and still was, but Abby's patience had seemingly expired. There was a charged energy in the room. Gone was Rylan's flirting and Abby's gentle coaxing. She was going in for the kill.

"I finished," Rylan said in a flat tone. "You set a deadline and I met it."

He pushed a report across the table. A letter attached to a thick binder with folded blueprints tucked inside.

Abby didn't touch it. "I thought so."

"The project has been approved. There are no more impediments to getting started on the work." Rylan couldn't have sounded less excited if he were talking about toothpaste.

Spence was pretty sure he'd missed a step. No question the Abby-Rylan dynamic had flipped. Rylan actually looked a little afraid of her, which was probably a wise choice. Abby walked into the meeting looking all professional and no-nonsense in her trim black suit. Rylan usually let his gaze travel a bit. He'd wait until she turned and would sneak a few peeks. Not today.

Spence found the outfit sexy as hell. That little bit of light blue stuck out from the top of her buttoned jacket had sent his control careening into a wall. He'd seen the jacket unbuttoned earlier in her office. He knew the shirt was silky and thin and all he wanted to do was get his hands under it.

He really hoped he earned that right back soon.

"If that's all?" Rylan stood up before he finished the sentence.

"You've signed everything?" Abby just stared at the man, still not touching the paperwork she'd pushed so hard to get completed. "I don't want any surprises."

"No, we're done."

She nodded. "Good answer."

A minute later, he was packed up and Spence showed him out the door. Handed him off to an assistant, then stepped back into the conference room. The satisfied grin on Abby's face suggested she liked how that battle ended.

"Want to clue me in?" he asked.

Her head jerked up. "What?"

"That was a big change in attitude. You were coddling him, letting him take the maximum time to ensure the project got approved. It's exactly what I would have done since Rylan seems like the type who craves attention." Minus the flirting, of course. Spence was pretty sure Rylan wouldn't have tried that tactic on him. Spence leaned against the table and faced her where she still sat in the chair. "He went from drooling over you and dragging his feet to jumping to your every demand."

She shrugged. "We had a chat and I made my position clear."

"Which means?"

"I told him he had misstepped if he thought he had

a chance at something with me. Also made it clear I wanted the job done."

"Uh-huh." That sounded like half a story to Spence. "Did he actually make a pass at you?"

A week ago that question might have sent her temper spiking. It could have led to a fight, with one of them storming out. But that had changed, too. Spence no longer weighed every word. He was careful but not wary.

She stood up. Let her hand trail over his thigh. Low enough to be decent but with enough pressure to pull his mind away from the office. "Abby..."

"I made it clear that it would be stupid for him to try anything." She rubbed her thumb back and forth over a crease in his pants.

"Are you trying to prove to me that you can handle him?"

"Didn't I?"

"You did, but I already knew that you would." His hand went to her waist and he toyed with one of the buttons holding the sides of her jacket together. "Any chance I can convince you to skip your meeting and have lunch with me?"

By "lunch," he meant not eating. He'd settle for an actual meal, but his control was wavering. The more he watched her in action at work and cuddled with her on the couch at night, the more he wanted everything. And the more Jackson's use of the word *love* didn't seem so misplaced. Not that he was ready to talk about that, because he wasn't.

"Derrick would be impressed with your work ethic," she said.

Spence and Derrick had an understanding. Spence knew his strengths and Derrick didn't try to redirect those. "My skills tend to be best used in going out and getting us new projects to bid on, or better yet, just win outright."

"Always the salesman."

"It takes a lot of time and study." He stood up, letting his hand linger on her stomach. "Weeks, sometimes months, of reviewing everything to find the right course of action."

"Are we still talking about work?"

Not really. "Of course."

She tugged on the bottom of his tie. "How about this. We both be good employees this afternoon, then we'll meet up for dinner."

He liked the way her mind worked. "I can make a reservation."

"At my place." She skimmed a finger down the buttons of his shirt. "We'll stay in."

All the blood rushed from his head. The idea of a night with her, even just holding her, sounded so good. "You sure?"

"I hear you're very skilled at doing dishes."

He had to smile at that. She could charm and seduce him into just about anything. "Not to brag but I'm good at a lot of things."

"I plan to let you prove that to me."

With one battle done, Abby moved on to the next one. Last week, as soon as her bad cold passed, she'd called Rylan. Made it clear to him that passing notes to her from other businessmen was both juvenile and a move guaranteed to haunt him. She mentioned filing a complaint. Then she talked about telling Spence about what really happened and how Rylan let Jeff Berger use him.

She'd dropped every threat she could think of to teach him a lesson. Once she had his full attention, telling him he had exactly one week to finish his work and deliver his report had been easy, and he beat her deadline by a few days.

She suspected this meeting with Jeff would not run as smoothly.

They met in a noisy restaurant. One of those impossible-to-get-reservations type in a building that used to be a bank or a warehouse or something. It had soaring ceilings and the bar stretched out along one side with an open kitchen in the back.

The servers shared a similar look. She thought of it as unshaven, hair-in-a-bun male Pacific Northwest vibe. It fit with the decor and the all-black serving outfits. They seemed to know Jeff and hovered around the table, trying to please him. Even called him by name.

She wrote the whole scene off as more of his power-play antics. He wanted to impress her, make her think he controlled everything. Whatever.

What he didn't understand is she'd already taken

on Eldrick and Rylan this week and somehow managed to tame Spence into potential boyfriend material at the same time. Whatever threats Jeff had planned would be just one in a long line she intended to bat down.

She ignored the menu in front of her and reached for the water glass. Taking a sip, she glanced around the main dining room. Saw the plates of salad and bottles of wine being delivered to tables. Heard the clink of silverware as she tried to decipher the mumble of conversation around her.

Jeff's heavy sigh broke through the action. He slipped an envelope across the table. "Here is an explanation of what we need and compensation for your time. Just as we discussed."

"We never discussed anything."

He frowned at her. "Don't play hard to get."

The man was savvy. Abby guessed there was a typed note and cash in there. Didn't matter because she didn't intend to open it and find out. She slid it back across the table in his direction. "Not interested."

Jeff made a big show of folding his menu and putting it aside. He leaned in with his elbows on the edge of the table. "Now, Abby. You don't even know what I'm offering."

Turned out this meal was exactly what she thought it was about—trying to get her to spy on Jameson Industries. She wasn't interested in anything from Jeff but she sure wasn't interested in that.

"A trip to nowhere." She looked around for the

restroom. From there she could make an easy escape. That sounded smarter than risking Jeff making a scene. "No, thanks."

She turned in her chair and started to get up.

Jeff's hand clamped down on her wrist. "Sit down."

She didn't jerk back or start yelling. Didn't give him the satisfaction of knowing his touch made her want to throw up the stale protein bar she'd choked down before coming into the restaurant fifteen minutes ago. "Amazing how you become less charming when you don't get what you want."

"I tried this the nice way. I offered you a job months ago, and you said no. I just offered you an easy way to make extra money and you pushed it away." He dropped her wrist and sat back again. "Do you see what I'm saying?"

She refused to rub her wrist to alleviate the burning sensation of his hold. "That you can't take no for an answer."

"You're the problem here, Abby."

She was just about done with overbearing businessmen. Seeing how others operated made her appreciate Derrick and Spence's style even more. No wonder Eldrick had thought he could get away with bullying. Apparently, it was the go-to move for many just like him.

But the comment did intrigue her. She gave in to her curiosity. Maybe this way she could prepare for whatever he had planned for the future. "How do you figure that?"

"I'm done losing to Derrick." Jeff shook his head. "All I need is some information. Not on every job, of course. That would look suspicious."

In other words, Jeff couldn't compete on a fair playing field. Good to know. "I work there. Screwing him screws me."

"You have a safety net in my office in the form of any managerial position you want. I'll make up a title for you."

Right, because that's how this worked. Once she broke the trust in one office, her reputation would be in shambles. No one would hire her, not even Jeff. But that didn't even matter because she wasn't tempted. Just because Jeff was that type didn't mean she was.

He'd made a similar offer at the lowest point in her business career. She'd been harassed and just lost Spence. Felt vulnerable and convinced she'd be fired. She guessed she'd given off a pathetic vibe. But still, she didn't bite then. She had no idea why Jeff thought she would now.

"You're asking the wrong person. I don't play like this." She had pride and integrity and didn't plan to forfeit either.

"You're going to regret this." Jeff stared at the untouched envelope then picked it up again. Slipped it in his jacket pocket.

"The lunch? I already do."

"We'll see how funny you think this is after…"

After what? She was dying to know. "Goodbye, Jeff."

She got up and forced her legs to move. Something about his tone and that last comment pulled at her as she walked away. The words could mean anything. But she'd learned early to expect the worst. Now she did.

Eleven

Spence followed her home that night. Abby left about fifteen minutes before he did because he got stuck on a phone call about a problem with a project at the University of Maryland. One of those calls he couldn't just jump off of because there were ten other bored people in on it who also wanted to get off the line.

The second after he hung up, he raced out of the office. Tried to act professional and nod and smile to everyone he passed in the office hallway but his insides churned. He'd heard the whispers about him dating Abby. Even spoke with Derrick about them. The conclusion was that Human Resources should talk to Abby to make sure she was okay. People dated. He and Abby knew the dangers because they'd already lived through them once. Mostly.

That left a clear line between him and Abby tonight. Except for the ongoing trust issues, his idiot father and the very real sense she was hiding something from him. All of those issues stayed stacked in a teetering tower between them, but Spence was ready to unpack.

He also ached to touch her again. Once had not been enough. The hurried sex in the pantry could only be described as explosive. He wanted to experience the joy of slowly getting to know her body. And that could happen tonight…unless he misread the cues, in which case dinner worked, too.

She'd slipped him a note with the security code for the garage and the number of the space to park in. Then, Abby being Abby, she re-sent the information by text. The numbers mixed with his memories of the pantry and clouded in his brain, but he managed to get inside the gate.

The elevator turned out to be tougher because it required the guy at the desk to call up and get permission from Abby to let him in. For one tense second, he worried she'd changed her mind and would say no, but the guy waved him up.

That was five minutes ago. Now he got off the elevator and shot Jackson's front door a quick look. Having him so close by rattled Spence but he pretended it wasn't a big thing.

He raised his hand to knock on Abby's door right

as it opened. She stood there, hair falling over her shoulders and a welcoming smile on her face.

He almost lost it.

Somehow he managed to lean in for a quick kiss. Even the slight touch of their lips had his heart racing until the echo of it thumped in his ears. He stepped inside the condo and closed the door behind him. After turning the lock, he followed her inside the open space.

The condo was new, with top-end everything. Her bedroom sat shadowed off to the right. He tried not to think about that room. Keeping his mind off the floor plan proved easy because he had something else—something much more interesting—to focus on right now.

Abby walked from the entryway through to the living room with those impressive hips swaying as she stepped. The drapes were drawn on the floor-to-ceiling windows behind her couch. Lamps lit the area in a soft glow. And she was wearing a dress. She'd been in a suit all day. He remembered because he'd thought about her skirt and the way it rode up her thighs, just a touch, as she walked.

The dress was solid red and bold. It wrapped around her with a same-color tie at her waist. He'd never seen it before but he was a fan.

As she stood there, her head tilted to the side and her hair cascaded over her shoulder. "Are you hungry?"

"Starving." He wasn't even sure if he could choke down food right now, but it seemed like a good answer. Logical in light of the time of night and the agreement they had to find food.

She made a humming sound. "That's a shame."

The list of take-out restaurants running through his brain slammed to a halt. "Excuse me?"

That smile, wide and inviting. Man, there was no way he was going to survive that. The seductive curve of her lips promised excitement. Or maybe he was still daydreaming. He honestly couldn't tell.

Reality blended with fantasy when he looked at her. Long legs and that face. Big eyes, full lips...yeah, he was lost. He had no defense against her.

She kept her hands at her side as she walked over to him. He would have moved but he was pretty sure his feet were welded to the floor. No part of him even flinched except the growing bulge in his pants. He really hoped that didn't make her twitchy. Another few minutes of her staring and she would notice. She couldn't *not* notice.

After a few yanks, she undid his tie and slipped it off his neck. Her fingers went to the buttons at the very top and opened two. When she slipped her hands inside the opening and placed her warm palm against his chest, he jumped. Couldn't help it.

"Are we eating?" The question sat out there. He sounded like he'd never had sex before, and he had. Plenty of times. But he didn't want to take a wrong turn here. He really wanted her to lead and take them down that hallway to her bedroom.

"You did say you were starving." She slipped

her thumb up his throat to the bottom of his chin. Brushed it back and forth.

That touch fueled him. Spun him up and readied him for more.

"I can't remember what I said." He wasn't sure how he drove there without crashing the car.

"When?"

"Ever."

"That thing you do where you lose your speech when you touch me?" She leaned in and ran her tongue along the top of his ear then whispered, "Very sexy."

His cells caught on fire. He could smell her shampoo and feel her soft hair skim over his cheek. And that body. She leaned in, pressing her chest against his and his brain misfired.

"I don't want to misread…"

"I like when you're careful but you need to catch up here." She bit down on his earlobe as she talked. Not hard but enough to get his attention.

The whisper of her voice echoed around him. He pulled back and looked at her. His gaze traveled over her face, looking for any sign of hesitancy. The blush on her cheeks and heat of her skin said yes. When her tongue peeked out, licked over his bottom lip, he may have said something. Who knew?

She shifted slightly and got a hand between them. With her fingers on that tie around her waist, she tugged. The belt came undone and the material keeping the dress closed slid open, revealing miles of perfect skin. She wore a pink bra that pushed her breasts up until they spilled over the tops of the cups and a tiny scrap that he guessed qualified as bikini bottoms.

It was a miracle his legs held him. Every thought about taking it slow left his head. Ran right out of there.

"I'm going to dream about this dress." He really wanted to buy her a thousand more like it. She could pick the colors. He did not care.

"About getting me out of it, I hope." With a shrug of her shoulders, she let the material slide off and fall to the floor with a swish. It pooled around her bare feet. Covered the soft purple polish covering her toes.

That choking sensation? He was pretty sure he swallowed his tongue. "Most definitely."

His words sounded garbled and a strange layer of fuzziness clogged his head. Whatever control he normally had he'd forfeited when he walked in the door.

A deep inhale didn't help. Neither did a silent count to ten. So, he gave in and touched her. Reached out and wrapped his arms around her. Lifted her off the floor and sighed in relief when her thighs clamped down against the outsides of his legs.

"It is unreal how sexy you are." Babble filled his brain, so he wasn't a hundred percent sure what he'd said, but she smiled.

Fingers slipped through his hair as her other hand skimmed down his back. "Still hungry?"

The light bulb clicked on in his mind. He finally figured out she wasn't talking about food. "I'll show you in the bedroom."

Somehow he got them there. Walked backward for part of it. Knocked his arm against the door frame and bit back a curse. Once he righted himself, he started moving again. His elbow slammed into the wall as he searched for the light switch. Then it was on and all he could see was her face above him and the bedroom right behind her.

He didn't waste any time. He stepped up to the edge of the mattress and lowered her. Let her slip down his legs. As soon as she sat down, her fingers went to work on his belt then his zipper. He tried to breathe in, rushed to get air in his lungs as she lowered her head and took him in her mouth.

One swipe of her tongue. One press of her hand against him, fingers around him, and his control snapped. As gently as possible, he pulled her away from him. His hands shook with the need to throw her back on the bed, but she did it for him. With excruciating slowness, she leaned back. Pressed her back on the mattress and flung her arms out to her sides.

She winked at him. "Why are you still dressed?"

Good question. He nearly ripped his shirt off then yanked his pants down. Probably set a speed record in getting naked. Then he crawled up her body, rubbing against her, over her. The resulting friction had him gasping.

"Condom." He couldn't forget this time. He'd never gone without protection before her. Before Abby and that pantry.

He didn't regret it, but he could do better. He owed her that along with so many other things.

He scrambled off the bed as she called out his name. Man, he loved the sound of his full name on her lips.

"Spencer, what are you..." She smiled when she saw the condom in his hand. "Yes."

"We'll be more careful this time." While she was sick, he'd texted her about birth control and their failure to use any. She assured him she was on the Pill, but they'd agreed a repeat of that move was not smart.

"Why are you still talking?" she asked as she reached up and pulled him back on top of her.

He kissed her then. Let out all the pent-up need and desire and plowed them both under. Kissed her until the blood ran from his head and his lower half pulsed with the need to strip her underwear off and throw it on the floor.

When he lifted his head, she looked dazed. Smiling with swollen lips and big watchful eyes.

"You are so beautiful." He meant it. Every word.

He'd never had any woman break through his defenses and reach inside him like she had. Through everything, all the pain and distrust, he could never wipe her from his mind. Now he knew he didn't have to.

His hand slipped behind her back to unclip her bra. Peeling it off her was like unwrapping the best present. His breath caught in his throat as his mouth dipped to kiss her. He ran his tongue over her, around her nipples, and felt her fingers clench in his hair.

Slow. She deserved all of his attention for as long as he could handle it. But then her hand snaked down his body. Those fingers wrapped around his length. He had to rest his forehead against hers as he gulped in air and wrestled for control.

"Spencer." She brought her knees up until the inside of her thighs pressed against his sides. "Go faster."

The words pummeled him and the urge to give in grabbed him. But this was for her. Tonight, and for as many nights as she would give him. "Soon."

He moved down her body, kissing a trail over her bare skin. Loving every inch of her softness, each curve. He reached her stomach and pressed a kiss on the slight bump he found so sexy. When she gasped, he did it again.

Turning his head to the side, he rubbed his cheek against her bare skin. "You are perfect."

"You…" Her back arched off the bed and those heels dug into the mattress.

There, sprawled out with her chest rising and falling on harsh breaths, she silently called out to him. Looked so inviting.

His mouth dipped lower. A finger slipped inside her as she shifted on the bed. He circled and caressed until her thighs clenched against his shoulders. He would never get a clearer sign of how ready she was, and he didn't wait for one.

Up on his knees, he rolled on the condom. Then his body slid over hers again. He pressed inside. Keeping his thrust slow and steady, he pushed until her body tightened around his. His brain, his muscles—every part of him—begged for release. But he held back. He needed to know she'd gotten there before he let go.

Her breaths came in pants now. Her exposed neck enticed him as her head pressed deep into the pillows. She grabbed the comforter, balling it in her fists. With every second, her control slipped further away and it was amazing to watch.

Her skin glowed as sweat gathered on his forehead. Pressure built inside him, clawing at him. Still, he didn't give in. He slipped his hand between their bodies. Touched her as he pumped in and out.

The trembling started in her legs. He could feel the muscles vibrate against him as the pulses started moving through her. Her hips lifted and her hands grabbed on to his shoulder. He waited until the last second, until she gasped and her body bucked, before he gave in to his own orgasm. It rolled through him, wiping everything else out.

For those few minutes, it was just him and her and the rhythm pounding in his head as he pushed into her. When the explosion came, all he could do was ride it out. Hold on to her, wrap his body around hers and give himself over to it.

It took a bit more time for his body to calm and the pulsing to stop. Reality came back to him in pieces. Her fingers brushing over his shoulder lured him in. He buried his face in her shoulder and inhaled. He'd get up, move—do something. Soon. But not yet…

* * *

He didn't know how long he rested with her on the bed with his eyes closed. It really didn't matter since she'd curled into his side with her hand on his chest. He slipped his palm up and down the soft skin of her arm, loving the feel of her.

This felt right. He'd ached for this, dreamed about it, got angry that he couldn't stop thinking about what this might feel like when he left. Being away from her and adrift, not having any real direction, was the answer then. He'd needed to clear his head. Yeah, he got the facts wrong and blamed her instead of dumping it all on his father where it belonged. After those few stunned seconds, he'd been so willing to believe the man who raised him and always disappointed him. Spence knew now that he needed to break the habit.

He was about to drift off to sleep when she started talking. She leaned up on her elbow and stared down at him. "May I ask you a question?"

And that destroyed any chance of him sleeping, possibly ever. He couldn't think of a time when that question ended well. "Why do I think I should say no? I mean, I can only mess up from here, right?"

She smiled as her fingertip traced his lips. "You're not going to mess up."

"I like how much faith you have in me." He folded the arm that wasn't holding her behind his head. "Go ahead."

"What are we?"

The wording was strange but he knew exactly what she meant. They'd spent every evening together since she got over being sick. He planned to repeat that pattern next week and for many after that. "You sure know how to lead with the big questions."

"There's gossip at work and—"

"Does that bother you?" Maybe he'd been too casual about the boss thing. He'd taken himself off all of her projects. He would be there if she needed to consult but they restored Derrick as her direct line of supervision. It was neater that way. A separation of work and private life. Better for her in case she did have an issue.

"Not if whatever is between us is real."

The words beat back the anxiety welling inside of him. He had an easy answer for this. "It's real."

"Are you just saying that?" Her eyes narrowed but amusement still lingered in her voice.

Despite her light tone, he took the question very seriously. "Because we're naked and in your bed and I'm hoping I get to stay here? No. I'm saying the words because they're true. Because they've been true and probably were even back when I messed up and pushed you away."

She blew out a long breath as her hand came to rest on his chest again. "I hate what happened to us back then."

Now was the right time for the apology. Nothing fancy. Just the truth.

"I'm sorry. Sorry I didn't listen or trust you." He brushed her hair off her cheek. "Sorry I didn't punch my dad in the face."

"I don't want to come between you."

Spence almost laughed at that. Might have if she didn't look so serious. "Not possible. There's no relationship to ruin. Not anything meaningful."

"Don't say that."

Spence refused to get into that argument now. She was decent and loving and probably thought Eldrick might have some good hidden down deep inside him. Spence knew better. Even with Beth's coaxing, Eldrick would never be a guy Spence trusted around Abby. Not again.

He needed her to understand Eldrick wasn't between them. "But this—us—it is worth saving."

Her eyes got all shiny. "So, we're in this."

A lump clogged his throat, but he swallowed it down. "We're in it."

Her mood switched again. This time to playful as she climbed on top of him. Straddled his hips.

"Good. Now we can have dinner." She poked him in the chest. "I seem to remember you owing me a burger."

"At your service, ma'am."

Twelve

The next week passed in a haze of happiness. A voice in Abby's head told her to be careful, not to let herself enjoy it too much because it could be snatched away so quickly.

She'd never gone for long stretches without something going wrong. Like, spectacularly wrong. A bad boyfriend, a huge problem at work. Having to move. A huge expense she hadn't prepared for. Running out of money. Until she'd found stability with her job at Jameson, the last two years had been a constant strain.

Just to be safe, the only thing she'd spent any money on since she started receiving the big paycheck was her condo. She figured she always could sell it if finances grew tight again. It was her rainy-day fund, in a way.

Looking around the dining room table now, she couldn't call up any of those bad memories or nagging worries. Probably had something to do with how loud the Jameson family was. Man, they could talk about *anything*. Carter, specifically, was a pro at talking.

They'd all gathered to celebrate the news from Ellie's doctor that she could move around a bit more. She came back from her appointment two days ago and declared a family dinner was in order. Verbally walked all over Derrick's objections and made it happen. To make her happy, and everyone seemed determined to do that, they gathered.

Even now they passed a roast, vegetables and potatoes around the long rectangle table in Derrick and Ellie's dining room. Dishes clanked as Carter and Jackson argued about the benefits of mashed potatoes over all other potato dishes. Jackson's sister and Ellie's best friend, Vanessa, couldn't make it on short notice, and Ellie's brother was away at some computer seminar, but everyone else was there.

"Are you okay?" Spence whispered the question in Abby's ear as he leaned in closer.

She reached out and slid her hand over his thigh. Gave it a little squeeze. It was tempting to drive him a little mad under the table, but really, she wanted to keep the connection. After their week together, she'd been spoiled. She hated any distance between them outside of work.

This sensation of falling and being caught was new to her. So foreign but not unwelcome. Her young life centered on her and her mom. They had been an inseparable pair. Then she widened her circle to include a few friends. Now, with Spence, she opened it again for this makeshift family that joked with her while enveloping her in its incredible warmth.

He kissed her temple. "I know you're not used to so many people."

Carter snapped his fingers. He sat directly across from Abby and pointed at the dish next to Spence. "Stop licking your girlfriend and pass the peas."

Spence made a groaning sound. "Are you sad because you don't have a girlfriend?"

"We should find him one," Derrick said as he forked the meat off the tray then kept passing.

From his seat at one end of the table, he looked like a king presiding over his lands. Abby thought that might have been a scarier idea and his dominance might have carried more weight if he didn't spend half of the meal making lovey eyes at Ellie at the other end of the long table. He'd protested sitting so far apart but Ellie assured him he'd have the best view that way.

Honestly, Abby found the two of them adorable-bordering-on-annoying. Spence once talked about the bumpy road they had to engagement. She'd been in the office, but Derrick wasn't really one to drag his home life in. He hadn't before Ellie, anyway.

Not wanting to fall behind on the verbal poking going around the table, Abby leaned across Spence and looked at the one person at the table who seemed to keep eating no matter what happened around him. "Jackson, what's your sister's dating status?"

Jackson didn't even look up from his plate. "Nope."

"Come on." Carter laughed. "But she already loves me."

Jackson glared at Carter before glancing over at Abby. "I work with this crowd. Do you think I want to be related to them?" He froze for a second, then held up the hand that just happened to be holding his knife. "No offense."

Derrick snorted. "How could we possibly be offended by that?"

"I like them." Abby leaned in closer to Spence, soaking in his body heat. "You've all grown on me."

Spence slipped his hand around her and gave her lower back a gentle massage. "Thanks, babe. And the feeling is mutual."

Abby didn't know how he planned to eat with one hand attached to her, but that was his problem. She savored the touching and the food. She was about to ask Ellie how she'd made the meal when she was still confined to bed or sitting down for most of the day, but then common sense kicked in. The two women in the kitchen when they all arrived at the house likely did all the work. Clearly there were some benefits of eating at a Jameson home.

The money—the stunning breadth of it—still didn't sit right with Abby. She wasn't used to all that wealth. The Virginia house looked like a school when she'd driven up for the party. Derrick's town house was nothing short of spectacular but still managed to feel homey, which she credited to Ellie's handiwork.

Abby had been raised with so little. She appreciated every last shoe in her closet and can in her pantry. She'd picked each item out and purchased them. The only thing that kept her from fidgeting when she thought about the reality of Jameson money was that Spence never showed any sign of being impressed with his bank account. If he had, she would have balked.

"You have pet names for each other. Cute." Carter sent Spence a bug-eyed look. "The peas, Spence."

Spence didn't move. "You have legs."

"If I have to get up, I'm punching you."

"You're both annoying." Jackson picked up the bowl and passed it across the table to Carter.

He dug right in. "About time."

Through the controlled chaos, Derrick let out a loud exhale. Abby never knew her dad but she assumed this was the ultimate dad move. Make a noise and get everyone at the table listening. *Smooth.*

"This nonsense is going to stop when the baby comes," he said.

"We'll be too busy fighting over who gets to hold him to argue about anything else," Spence said as he tried to steal the bowl of peas back.

Carter moved it out of reach.

Ellie eyed them all over the top of her water glass. "Or her."

"Speaking of which—" Carter cut into his roast

"—are you still trying to sell that faulty birth control story to explain your current state?"

"My pregnancy doesn't need to be explained," Ellie said, emphasizing each word.

"Carter." Abby was pretty sure Spence kicked his brother as he said his name.

Ellie wasn't quite as subtle. She fixed Carter with a you're-right-on-the-edge glare even though she looked like she was fighting back a smile. "Don't make me burn your clothes in the fireplace."

He winced. "Hormones?"

She waved a knife at him. "Don't test me."

Abby felt a fog roll over her. The conversation picked at a memory she'd shoved to the back of her brain. A piece of information she didn't want to deal with that now came screaming back to her.

The Pill. Sex. Antibiotics. She'd started taking the meds that were in her bathroom the second she started feeling sick. That happened before she had sex with Spence. Before, during and after.

Antibiotics and birth control pills were a bad combination. Still a long shot for getting pregnant, but it could happen. Some medications played with the effectiveness of the pill. When she climbed out of her sickbed and remembered that, she'd rechecked on the internet. The news was not as negative on the possibility of getting pregnant as she'd hoped.

Good grief. It wasn't possible…was it?

Abby tried to remember Ellie's list of pregnancy symptoms, all that she had to fight off and go through.

"Faulty birth control?" Abby didn't mean to say the words out loud, but they were the only ones in her mind right now.

"Is this appropriate dinner conversation?" Derrick asked.

"It is in this house." Spence shrugged as he made another grab for the peas and reached them this time.

His look of triumph over something so simple made Abby smile. Or it would have if she wasn't busy counting days on the calendar in her head.

"The pregnancy is high-risk because my IUD failed," Ellie explained. "It's still in there."

Carter whistled. "Damn, Derrick."

"I didn't do it."

Spence glanced at Derrick. "Well, technically…"

"It kind of depends what the 'it' is in that sentence." Jackson froze in the middle of moving the roast closer to him. "Is that the doorbell?"

The bell chimed a second time.

"Isn't everyone here?" Derrick asked the question to the room in general. He clearly didn't expect an answer because he was up and out of his chair, on the way to the door.

A terrible thought ran through Abby's head. She leaned in to whisper it to Spence. "If your father is back in town—"

Carter nearly dropped his water glass. "Don't even joke about that."

Footsteps echoed on the hardwood floor as Derrick walked back in. He held an envelope. He dropped it on the sideboard that ran half of the length of the impossibly long room. Never looked at it again.

"What was it?" Spence asked even though he didn't sound that interested in the answer.

"Delivery of work documents." Derrick's gaze flicked to Ellie as he sat back down. "Don't glare. I didn't tell anyone to send stuff here."

"Yet, someone did. Gee, I wonder why they thought it was an okay thing to do." She did not sound pleased.

Derrick winked at her. "You forget how important I am."

"That ego." Carter shook his head. "Unbelievable."

Jackson scooped up more potatoes. "Try working with him."

Carter glanced at her. She could feel the heat of his stare as the conversation bounced around her. She tried to keep up but the idea of a baby was stuck in her head now. She wanted to kick it out but it had grabbed hold.

"Abby? Do you have an opinion on that?" Carter asked.

She couldn't stop looking at Spence, imagining what their children might look like. If a kid would have his stubbornness.

When she realized the table had gone unusually quiet and everyone stared at her, she struggled to mentally rewind the conversation and come up with an answer. "Uh, no. I'm taking the Fifth."

The talking picked back up again. About food.

About work. About anything Carter could think of, or so it seemed.

Spence leaned in closer, brushing her hair back behind her ear. "You sure everything is okay?"

"Just thinking." And panicking and generally kicking her own butt for being so careless. She'd never done that before. With her luck, it would only take one time.

He smiled at her. "You can concentrate on anything with all this noise?"

"It's called conversation, Spence," Jackson mumbled under his breath.

Ellie groaned. "Enough talking. Eat."

"The pregnant woman has spoken." Derrick picked up his glass in a toast.

"You know, for that power to keep working, you're going to have to be pregnant all the time." Jackson flinched, which must have meant Ellie kicked him. She was right there, after all. "Hey!"

"I'm up to the challenge," Derrick said.

Some of the color drained from Ellie's face. "Let's start with one first."

Abby looked down at her plate. She really hoped she wasn't the one saying that a month from now.

It took another half hour to finish up and move the conversation into the living room. On Ellie's orders, the men cleared the table and argued during every second of their work as if they'd been sent into the mines to dig for coal.

Spence didn't mind helping out. He'd do dishes,

but he refused to do them alone. In Derrick's house, that usually wasn't necessary because family dinners meant he hired people to handle most of the work. With Ellie being less mobile, Derrick was interviewing for a full-time cook, but he had to do it behind her back because she was not comfortable with the idea.

Spence glanced into the great room next to where they'd eaten dinner and saw them all gathered around, lounging on sofas. Arguing, like they always did. He was pretty sure that was part of the Jameson gene pool. Jackson probably picked up the habit by association.

The only person not having coffee and debating dessert options was Abby. She stood in the doorway between the dining room and the great room, watching. He'd picked up on her mood change earlier. His family could be overwhelming. He got that. But he sensed something else was bothering her.

They'd been growing closer, spending more time together. Talking about things other than work. He didn't want her to shut down now.

"You sure you're okay?" He slipped his arms around her waist and pulled her body back against his. "You got quiet."

She sighed. "That was a lot of activity."

"Yelling. A meal with this group is a lot of yelling."

When she leaned against him, he put his chin on her shoulder. Breathed, letting this moment settle inside him. The comfort of it made him think he misread her earlier. The slight tension running through her had vanished. Now she relaxed.

She rubbed her hand over his arm. "You love it."

He couldn't deny it. Today was the kind of event that drew him back to DC. Being able to unwind with them. Joke and have fun without fear of someone losing their temper or their dad storming in. "I kind of do."

"Was it like that growing up?"

"Hell, no." He thought about the right way to explain it. He wasn't asking for pity or suggesting he had it bad, not compared to other people. But it hadn't been good, either. "We weren't allowed to talk at the table."

She turned around in his arms to face him, never breaking contact. "Are you kidding?"

The concern was evident in her eyes. Healthy concern. He could handle that.

He brushed his fingers through her hair, loving the feel of it. "Does Eldrick strike you as a guy who wanted to hear what his kids had to say?"

She rolled her eyes. "My mom would come home exhausted and still listen to me babble."

She shared so little about her past and her life before. From the few bits she'd dropped, Spence had an image in his mind. She liked solitude and trusted very few. That probably was a smart way to live. At least it seemed safer.

But he did miss having someone who knew more about her and might be able to offer some advice to him now and then. Ellie only offered up so much. "I'm sorry I never got a chance to meet your mom."

"Me, too."

He hugged her then. Pulled her in close and wondered how he'd ever let go of her in the past. That had been a terrible mistake, maybe his worst. And that was saying something.

He spied the envelope that was delivered earlier. He'd forgotten about it. Since it lay there untouched, he guessed Derrick had, too. Spence almost reached for it now. He had no idea what could be so important for a home delivery. Then he saw the return address. "Jeff Berger."

Abby froze in his arms. "What?"

Not wanting to let go of her, Spence nodded in the direction of the envelope. "The delivery was from him. The guy has this weird competition thing with Derrick."

Her expression stayed unreadable. "Why?"

"When Derrick saved the company, he did it by grabbing a bunch of small jobs, then expanding the business into new areas, both geographic and different types of projects." Everything had been a struggle back then. Spence was relieved they'd moved past those days. "He cut right into Berger's business and Jeff took it personally and has been looking for revenge ever since."

Abby's hands slid down Spence's arms. Her fingers slipped through his. "Wow."

"It's a stupid guy thing. Jeff gets spun up even higher because Derrick won't engage."

She frowned. "Then why was Jeff at the party?"

"Keep your enemies close." At least that's what

Spence assumed. He hadn't bothered to ask because he didn't care that much about Jeff.

"I hate that saying." An edge moved back into her voice.

He decided to let it go. She'd tell him when she was ready. "But it's smart."

"Unfortunately, yes."

She was frowning again but Spence had the perfect temporary solution. "We need cake."

"My hero."

Thirteen

The sun streamed through her bedroom windows early the next morning. The sheers blocked most of the harsh light, leaving the room bathed in a hazy glow. Shadows moved across her beige walls. She tried to concentrate, to keep her eyes open and watch the play of shape, but they kept drifting shut.

Blame Spence. His expert mouth and those hands were at fault. His fingertips slipped over her as he placed a trail of kisses over her inner thigh. When his mouth reached the very heart of her, her hips angled forward, giving him greater access.

Heat pounded her as she shifted on the mattress. Her skin felt tingly, as if every nerve ending had snapped to life. The coolness of the room blew over her bare skin but she barely felt it. Not while Spence's warmth surrounded her.

Her hand dropped down and her fingers tangled in Spence's hair. She lifted her head to get a better view. The sight of him there, snuggled between her legs, had a breath stuttering in her chest. He was naked and confident. That finger worked magic as it slipped inside her.

"Spence..." she said his name on a soft puff of air.

Without breaking contact with her body, he glanced up. She could see those eyes as his mouth worked on her. The tightening inside her kept ratcheting up, bringing her closer to the edge. The orgasm hovered just out of reach. She tried to clamp down on those tiny inner muscles. Bring his finger in deeper and hold it there. But Spence had other ideas. He flipped her over until she landed on her stomach.

"Yes. Please." Her body begged for his touch. Forget playing games, she wanted more and depended on him to give it to her.

His hand smoothed down her back. Started at the base of her neck and traveled the whole way to the dip in the very small of her back. The trail sparked life into her exhausted body. Energy surged through her one more time. She separated her legs, hoping he'd get the hint, but he just kissed her. Pressed his lips to the base of her spine.

The touch was sexy. So seductive.

But enough. She twisted until her lower body stayed pressed to the mattress where he straddled her. Her top half turned to face him. "You are playing a dangerous game."

"Just enjoying a lazy morning." But that smile suggested he knew exactly what he was doing to her.

"Oh, really?" She pulled her legs up, tucking them close to her chest, and sat up.

His eyebrow lifted. "I thought you wanted to be touched."

"On your back."

Fire flashed in his eyes. His body practically pulsed with excitement. She was pretty sure she saw his hands shake as he lowered his body down. He rested on his back with his knees in the air and his feet flat against the bed.

"Well?" The challenge was right there in his voice. *Silly man.* "Maybe I should take my time."

She sat next to him and dragged her finger up his thigh to his hip bone. Avoided the place he most obviously wanted to be touched. When he lifted his hips, pushing his growing length closer to her hand, she continued on to his stomach. Skimmed her palm over the firm muscles there. The ridges were so pronounced. So sexy.

"Abby, I'm dying here." His voice sounded strained.

She loved that reaction.

Making sure to brush her body against his, she reached over him. Dipped down so her breasts pressed against him, but only for a second. He reached for her, but she'd grabbed the condom off the nightstand and sat back up.

Holding the packet, she hesitated. Memories of the dinner and the medication issue came rushing back at her. She thought about what could be and the decisions they'd have to make.

Then his thumb trailed over her thighs and slipped between her legs. "Hey, you okay?"

She heard the note of concern in his voice. Saw his eyes start to narrow. They would talk, but not now. She bent over him and pressed her mouth against his in a kiss that reassured him everything would be fine. In that moment, she believed it.

She opened the packet and unrolled the condom over him. Didn't waste another second thinking or debating. Not when he was right there and so ready.

She lifted one leg and straddled his hips. Pressed her palm against his chest. Her other hand went to his length. The slightest touch had his hips lifting, as if seeking out more. And she gave it to him.

She pushed up on her knees and fitted her body to his. Relaxing down, she let him slide into her. The connection, that friction had her heartbeat skipping again. Pressing on his chest, she lifted her body again. Slow and deliberate, she pulled up until they almost separated, and then she plunged down again.

The movement, the up and down, had her breath hitching in her chest. She squeezed her thighs together and heard him moan. With their bodies wrapped around each other, touching in so many places, every shift she made sent a vibration racing through him. She welcomed the surge of power that moved through her.

His hands slipped to the back of her thighs. His fingers clenched against her skin. "I need you to move."

It was so tempting to draw out the sweet torture. She tried for a few more seconds, but got caught in her own trap. Her heartbeat thundered in her ears and their joint breathing echoed around the room. The heated skin and slow thrust of his body into hers had that tension winding inside her again. Every muscle tightened as her head fell back.

She let her hair drop down her back. Dug her fingernails into his skin, imprinting marks on his chest. A wild need fueled her now. An almost primal need to get closer, to feel his body buck under hers.

His hands settled on her hips and he held her there. Kept her suspended on her knees as he lifted his hips up and down. That final move had her head spinning. The building inside her spilled over. The orgasm hit her before she was ready but right when she needed it. Raw and pulsing, her body let go.

She closed her eyes, enjoying the sensations riding her. Feeling him tense under her. She knew he was close and tightened her thighs on either side of his waist to make it happen. Then they both lost it. Their breaths mixed and their muscles shook. She came and he got there right after her.

There were words she needed to say. But her mind couldn't hold a thought. Whatever it was would have to wait until breakfast, or at least until her brain restarted. Until then she could close her eyes again.

She sank down, curling up on his chest. Loving the feel of his strong arms as they wrapped around her. Their bodies were joined and hot. They should head for the shower. That needed to happen…

She drifted off to sleep.

Two hours later, he walked around her kitchen, cursing her for not having milk in the house. She drank her coffee black and professed a general disdain for milk. She insisted adults didn't have a big glass of the stuff with any meal. She wasn't wrong about that part, but a guy needed certain things in his morning beverage.

Thanks to the sex, he was willing to let the oversight slide this time. Probably every time.

He turned around and leaned against the cabinet next to the stove. His gaze moved over the condo. From here, he could see the living area and catch a peek of the unmade bed they just crawled out of down the hall to the left. Another bathroom and bedroom sat on the right side of the condo. He barely ventured over there because he had no intention of sleeping separate from her.

The sectional caught his attention. The thing was not small. She mentioned something about wanting a couch that could function as a bed when she was too lazy to get up. A place she could curl up and watch movies. He wasn't entirely sure what that meant but from the pillows stacked on it and on the floor around it, and that blanket rolled up in a ball, he couldn't deny his love of relaxing on it with her.

"Good morning." She walked into the kitchen

wearing a pair of shorts and a slim-fitting T-shirt. It had a tiny dog with big eyes on it.

He appreciated the outfit. It might be his second favorite, next to that red wrap dress. That thing went in his clothing Hall of Fame. He seriously considered wading into her walk-in closet to find it and move it to the front as a hint.

She was barefoot and those legs went on forever. Much more of this and they'd be back in that bedroom for round three.

She took his mug and grabbed a quick sip. "Have you finally come to your senses and started drinking your coffee black?"

"You're out of milk."

"I don't buy it."

"Which should be illegal."

She took another sip. "I have that stuff you don't need to refrigerate."

She had to be kidding with that. "Woman, no."

"Fine." She smiled as she poured her own cup and joined him in leaning against the cabinets.

They both surveyed the condo. It was a quiet, relaxing morning. Not the way he was used to getting up but he hoped it became a habit.

"I need to ask you a weird question."

And then she ruined the peace with that comment.

"You have got to stop beginning conversations with that sort of phrase." He pretended to wipe his forehead. "I'm already sweating."

"The topic won't help."

Yeah, he needed to put down the breakable mug.

He set it on the counter and faced her, not sure what was about to hit him. "And?"

"We didn't use a condom the first time."

He let out some of the breath he'd been holding. They'd already been through this, but maybe she forgot because she was sick with a fever at the time. "I'm sorry. That was my fault."

She shook her head. "We were both there. We're both responsible for being...irresponsible."

That all sounded reasonable. "Okay. That's nice to hear but I admit I'm a bit lost because you're frowning and looking serious."

"What if I got pregnant?" The question rushed out of her.

He was happy he had a hold on the edge of the counter or he might have fallen to the floor. "Uh... is this hypothetical?"

"I'm serious."

He was terrified and his tongue might have gone numb. "I am, too."

"So?"

"Do you think you're pregnant?" He reached for her then. Put his hands on her waist and turned her until they stood only a few inches apart, facing each other head-on.

She put her mug down and rested her hands on his chest. "I don't know."

Not the answer he wanted...or maybe it was. He was new at this.

"Okay. Why do you think it's a possibility?" Because that had never entered his mind. They had sex without the condom and talked about it. About her being on the Pill and both of them always being careful until right then.

A new phase, a more responsible one, started. Now this.

"I was on antibiotics." She must have seen the confusion on his face because after a few beats of silence she continued talking. "The meds can mess with the Pill."

The comment triggered a memory. He'd known that. Somewhere in the back of his mind, he'd filed that information away, hoping never to need to use it.

He swallowed as he forced his voice to stay calm. Inside him was a wild frenzy. His brain skipped from question to question. His knees tried to fold. He wasn't completely sure he was still breathing. "Do you want to take a test?"

"We should."

She sounded so calm. How the hell was that possible?

"If you are..." He had no idea what to say next.

"Is that panic I hear in your voice?" A slight bit of anger vibrated in hers.

"No." Yes. Absolutely, yes. But they would get through it. "We'll handle it."

Her eyes narrowed and her body stiffened. "What does that mean?"

This was the one question he had the answer to. "We will do whatever you want us to do."

"Even if that means having the baby?"

His vision blinked out for a second. He looked at

his life as it stretched out in front of him. He'd never seen an image that included kids. For Derrick, sure. The guy was a born father. He was even great with Ellie's grown brother. But Spence wasn't convinced he possessed the skills. Looked like he'd be taking every class available to try to get up to speed.

Somehow, he would manage. That's what he did. That's what she and a baby would deserve. No matter how limited he might be, she would be great. And he could learn to be better than his father ever was.

He nodded. "Even then. We'll have the baby."

She still hadn't moved. "Get married?"

He had no idea where that came from, but as he stood there, he realized he viewed that as a package. "Yes."

She touched a finger to the corner of his mouth. "You look a little green."

Of course he did. Anyone would. No one should waltz into parenthood without at least a little panic. "Didn't you when you first realized this was a possibility?"

For a few more seconds, she just stood there, staring at him in silence. Finally, a small smile broke out on her lips. Some of the tension strangling the kitchen evaporated as she nodded. "Fair enough."

Not the words he'd use, but okay. "Abby, you can count on me."

He hoped that was true. He wasn't the guy who stuck around, but he would. They may have stumbled through their relationship so far, and still kind of were, but they would resolve all of their issues and concerns. And fast. He'd make her happy and do what they needed to do. But they were dealing in ifs and not facts.

"We definitely should take the test." *We* being her, and *test* meaning as many as he could find. There was no reason to believe one.

"Tomorrow."

He didn't understand the delay. "Why wait?"

"We're going to enjoy one more day of not knowing."

It hit him then. She really thought she was. She denied having symptoms…or had he asked that? The whole conversation was a blur. It would take days for him to unravel it and get his mind working again.

"If you want us to wait, we wait." It couldn't hurt anything. They would be so early. Not that he knew anything about babies or timing, because he didn't.

"You're a good man, Spencer Jameson."

He wasn't, but he was trying. For her. "Because of you."

"You give me too much credit." Her arms wound around his neck. The lightness in her voice suggested she'd dealt with the pregnancy information and had mentally moved on to the next topic.

He was not so lucky.

"You're the best thing that's ever happened to me." As he said the words, he realized he meant them. Without the pregnancy news, this is where he'd tell her he loved her. Because he did. He hadn't needed Jackson to tell him. Not really. The sensation that moved through him when he saw her, or even just heard her voice in the hallway, wasn't like anything he'd ever experienced. It filled him, made him feel whole.

But there was too much going on to say the words now. He didn't want one thing messed up with the other. When he said the words, he didn't want there to be any doubt why he did. That meant waiting, holding it inside for another few days, which was safer anyway. Once he said them, he wouldn't be able to call them back.

Her smile grew. "I am pretty great."

"And so modest."

She kissed him. Short and sweet. "And hungry."

"For food this time, right? I can fix that one right now." He pulled back, thinking to raid the refrigerator even though the idea of stepping outside for a few gulps of fresh air sounded good.

She caught his arm as he brushed past her. "Thank you."

Gratitude. He wasn't sure how he felt about that. Then again, he didn't feel much of anything at the moment. He was numb. "For?"

"Everything."

Fourteen

Abby didn't often get a summons to come to Derrick's office in the middle of the afternoon. He called her or sent a message. That worked best since she had a calendar full of meetings and phone calls, but she pushed everything for this meeting.

Now that the school renovation project was a go, she had about a hundred deadlines to set and people she needed to corral. Not that she minded. This was her favorite part, setting everything down and seeing the hard work turn into something real.

That's kind of how she thought of Spence. He'd stayed at her house for a string of nights. Settled in and looked right at home there on her couch. He'd even survived the baby talk this morning. She almost didn't. Her emotions had roller-coastered all over the place as she watched his facial expression change. Surprise to panic to should-I-run. The good news is that last one only came in a flash then was gone again.

But they needed to know the truth in case they had to make plans. No more guessing. She had two tests in her bag. Tonight they would have the answer.

Her stomach flipped at the thought. She'd held it together so far, but she was pretty sure she'd be bent over blowing into a paper bag no matter what the result was. The anxiety growing inside her guaranteed that.

Speaking of the possible future daddy…she looked up right as she turned the corner to the hallway leading to Derrick's office. Spence stood there. Tall and confident. The unexpected sight of him made her steps falter, but she quickly regained her balance.

"What are you doing?" She put her hand on his arm. Even thought about kissing him.

Despite the lack of traffic in this hall, she refrained from the public display of affection. It wasn't really her thing. They needed to keep a work–home life separation anyway. Human Resources had suggested a list of things they should do and not do. French kissing in the hallway had to be on there somewhere.

"Derrick asked to see me," Spence said.

Her hand tightened on Spence's arm. She didn't notice until his shirtsleeve bunched in her palm. "Me, too."

He frowned at that information. "Maybe Ellie?"

The thought tumbled in Abby's head. Her mind raced to the worst scenario. Just when she thought she'd stumbled on the worst, she came up with another. "Oh, no."

"It's okay." Spence put his hand over hers. The warmth on his skin seeped into hers. "He wouldn't be at work if something was wrong with her at home."

"Right." Derrick would burn marks in the carpet getting out of there and to Ellie. That's who he was.

But Abby got back to walking, just in case. Even picked up the pace a bit.

They passed by Jackson's office. His phone rang. The door was open but he wasn't at his desk. Not an unusual occurrence since he seemed to answer to everyone in the building. People called him for help and advice.

Derrick's door was open and she heard voices, both of them familiar. Carter mumbled something in an unusually serious tone. It was enough to get the worry churning inside her again.

Spence pushed open the door and they stepped inside. "What's going on?"

"We have a problem." Carter's gaze slipped to her as he spoke. "Close the door."

This couldn't be good. Closed-door meetings sometimes meant nothing, but the look on Carter's face—drawn and a bit pale—suggested this was big.

Spence shook his head. "What did Dad do now?"

Just the mention of him touched off a new bout of frustration inside her. Anger welled, ready to boil up and spill over. Eldrick had that effect on her and likely always would.

Carter continued to stare. A strange coldness

washed over Abby. She was so used to his smile and joking. From the minute she met him, she'd been struck by his genuine warmth. Derrick had to work at it. Spence tried to hide his. Carter was open and out there...but right now, he held his jaw stiff enough to crack.

Derrick dropped a large envelope on his desk. It had been opened and there was a note on top and photos spilled out. "It's not Dad."

Now he looked at Abby, too. The joint force of Derrick and Carter's angry attention only upped her anxiety levels. She handled stress fine but this crashed over her.

She mentally raced through every project, trying to think of what might have happened or gone wrong. It couldn't be the possibility of a new baby because she doubted Spence would have told them without knowing for sure or talking to her first. And she couldn't imagine either one of Spence's brothers having this reaction.

No, this was something else. Something fundamental that drove right to the heart of their loyalty to her and trust in her.

She looked at the familiar envelope. She couldn't place it, and then it hit her. The delivery at the family dinner. Jeff Berger, the big jerk.

"I don't understand what's going on," Spence said as he took a step toward Derrick's desk.

Carter kept his focus solely on her as he spoke. "Look at the photos."

Spence picked them up, filed through them, hesitating on the second before looking at them all again. With every movement, every shift, Abby felt her happiness drift away. Jeff had set her up. Somehow, he figured out how to get to Derrick. Worse, to Spence.

"What am I looking at?" Spence turned to her. "What are these?"

She couldn't avoid taking a turn now. She stepped up beside Spence and reached for the photos. Nothing in them proved to be much of a surprise. Her at the restaurant with Jeff. Jeff leaning in. His smile. It all looked intimate, so completely wrong and out of context to what really happened.

Never mind that she hadn't done anything wrong. That she'd turned Jeff down not once but twice. Several times, actually. She could feel the collective heat from the Jameson men's stares. It pounded down on her as she focused on the photos.

Jeff Berger was a piece of garbage. And he was determined to ruin her because she refused to dance at his command.

"There's a note." Derrick's voice sounded flat as he handed the sheet over to Spence then turned to her. "He says you approached him about working in his company. Offered proprietary information to him, saying he could expand and take us out of the market. He says he's warning me as a favor."

Her stomach dropped. She literally expected to see it hit the floor.

Her hands shook as she let the photos slip onto the desk. Denials and defenses crashed through her brain. She wrestled with the right thing to say, with how to explain what happened.

A warning as a favor. She wondered how long it took Jeff to come up with that gem. The man was a complete liar.

"Are you going to say anything?" Carter asked.

Derrick held up a hand. "Give her a second."

This time Carter snorted. "For what? She either has answers or she doesn't."

They were talking around her, over her. Derrick and Carter, but not Spence. All she cared about was his reaction. It took all of her strength to look at him.

She glanced over. Saw his wrinkled brow and eyes filled with confusion. Not hate or hurt, or anything like what seemed to simmer under the surface with Carter. No, Spence was struggling. She could see it on his face.

"It's not what you think." That wasn't the right thing to say but her brain refused to function. Her skin itched from being on display. Standing there in the middle of all of them having to defend herself... she hated Jeff for that. She would always hate him for that.

Spence hesitated for a second before he said anything. "Well, I think Jeff Berger is an ass."

Relief surged through her, but she tamped it down. She refused to get excited or believe that he wouldn't turn on her again. They had been through this sort of thing before. Denial mixed with disbelief.

"He insisted we meet." She left out the part about Rylan's role in all of this. He'd been complicit, but this part—all the trauma of this moment—was all on Jeff. This was about his vendetta against Derrick. The one she'd been dragged into the middle of and now had to fight her way back out of again.

"*He* did." Carter repeated.

She couldn't tell whether he believed her or not. Right now, the only thing that mattered was that they all listened. She needed Spence to step up and believe her. "Around the time you left, after the kiss and the mess with your father, Jeff contacted me. I was upset and frustrated and half convinced I was going to get fired…"

She stopped to catch her breath. She expected them to jump in and start firing questions at her, but they stayed quiet. They watched. Stood there taking it in with those matching blank expressions on their faces.

With no other choice, she pushed ahead. "I agreed thinking I might need to find another job."

Derrick frowned. "That was never a possibility. I begged you to stay."

"I know that now, but put yourself in my position. I'd fallen for a Jameson brother and now he hated me—"

Spence shook his head. "Abby, no. That was never true."

"Let her finish." Carter issued the order in a strangely soft voice as he sat on the edge of Derrick's big desk.

"It made sense that in a choice between me and

Spence—worse, between me and Eldrick—that I would lose. So, I was looking at other options."

"I would have done the same." It was the first positive thing Carter had said.

That glimmer of support spurred her on. "Well, Jeff did offer but he wanted business secrets and information on Derrick. I said no. I stopped taking his calls. Made every contact from his office run through my assistant first to make sure it was legitimate and work-related. He kept at it, checking in now and then. I ignored it all."

"But not forever." Spence pointed at the photos. "You wore that suit to work not too long ago. That restaurant is new. This is a recent meeting."

The accusation hung right there. There was nothing subtle about what Spence was saying. But he wasn't wrong, either. Denying the reality would only make things worse. Plus, she wanted to be honest.

She never intended to hide and sneak around with Jeff. He made that happen and she got pulled in. She'd take responsibility for not going to Derrick about the contacts, but the rest of this was a battle that wasn't even about her.

"He recently sent me a note demanding that we meet again. It had been months, so the contact didn't make sense. I ignored him again, but he was persistent. A bit threatening."

Carter slipped off the desk to stand again. "What?"

She rushed to explain. "Not physically. I never felt that."

"He cornered you at the engagement party." Spence exhaled. "You two were on the balcony."

She wasn't sure what the extra fact added. Spence's voice, his expression...he didn't give anything away. Doubts and concerns had to be spinning around inside him but he kept them all bottled up. Like the old Spence, he projected an outward calm while the storm raged.

That terrified her. Repressing could only mean bad things for them, for their future.

"He made it clear that our meeting would happen. Rather than fight it, I gave in." Her gaze traveled over them as she rubbed her hands together. Her skin was deathly cold. "Because I knew whatever he said wouldn't matter. I was never going to give him those secrets or work for him."

"What exactly did he want?" Derrick asked as he picked up his pen then put it down again.

"He didn't give specifics. He had an envelope for me but I refused to take it. I didn't even touch it because the whole meeting, the setup and nasty words, clearly were about wanting to get at Derrick and the company, and have an advantage in bidding. About winning contracts away from *us*." She added the emphasis to telegraph that they were in this together. Her loyalty stayed firmly with this company. Always. Even if she left, she'd never endanger what they'd built here.

"He's got a thing about Derrick." Carter shot his older brother an odd look. "You are going to have to confront him eventually."

Derrick nodded but didn't say anything.

"These photos." Spence fingered each one. "They look—"

"Staged." That was the right answer. She filled in the blank because if he suggested any other option she would lose it.

Her control hovered right on the edge. She wanted to open her mouth and yell at them. Surely they could see she'd been set up.

Spence nodded but his focus stayed on the photos. He paged through them one by one. Got to the last one then went back again. With every swipe of his hand, her fury built. It raced through her, fueling her.

"Clearly he had a photographer waiting." Anger vibrated in her voice.

Both Carter and Derrick watched her. Whatever they heard or saw had them both staring. Neither looked upset. It was more like they were analyzing her, testing her mood. Well, they didn't need to guess because she had every intention of unloading right now.

She slapped her hand over the photos, forcing Spence to look at her. "I have zero interest in Jeff and his bargains."

Spence nodded. "Okay."

Okay? "I said no because of you." She looked around at Carter and Derrick, too. "Because of all of you. Because I love this job, and I'm starting to love this family. And because being disloyal is not who I am. I can't believe I have to explain that to you."

Carter shook his head. "You don't."

For some reason that sent her temper flaring. "You believed the photos. When I walked in here, you thought I cheated on Spence or screwed over the company. Something."

"I read a note and saw some photos."

"And blamed me."

"Okay, hold it." Derrick held up both hands. "No one thinks you did anything. We wanted an explanation. It's clear this is Jeff being Jeff. I'm just sorry you got dragged into the middle of my garbage."

Her heartbeat still drummed in her ears. She wanted to believe that they saw the truth immediately. The rational part of her brain recognized that they had to go into this conversation wary and ask questions. But she was so tired of fighting. "I would never betray you."

Spence looked at her then. "Why didn't you tell me?"

The relief that had just started swirling through her petered out. "What?"

"We've been together nonstop. We've talked about other topics, very personal things. You never bothered to tell me about what Jeff did back then or what he was threatening you with now."

"So, this is my fault?"

The loudness of Spence's voice now matched hers. "I'm asking a simple question."

One that made her temper soar. He had a right to question. They did need to talk this through. She got all of that. But standing there, right then, in the middle of it all, she felt nothing but raw and hollowed out.

Instead of leaping to her defense along with Derrick
and Carter, Spence was still doubting her.

"He told me you wouldn't believe me."

"No, he's wrong." Spence shook his head. "I never
said that."

He didn't have to. She heard the words so clearly
in her head. "First your dad. Now Jeff. You never
believe me."

Spence reached out and held her arm by the elbow.
"Hey, that's not fair."

"When will I learn?" She pulled out of his grip.
"You know when? Right now. I'm going to finally
learn the lesson now."

The whole room vibrated from the force of her
slamming Derrick's office door as she stormed
out. Spence watched her go without saying a word.
Speech failed him. He didn't understand what just
happened. He'd been trying to reason it all out in
his mind, every step. The idea that Jeff Berger was
trying to push her around and she didn't tell him…
it made Spence sick. What kind of trust was that?

He took a step, thinking to go after her. Carter
blocked his path.

He loomed there. "You have a couple of choices
about what you do next."

One. There was only one choice and Spence was
about to do it. "I'm going to talk with her."

"Wrong one," Derrick said as he walked out from
behind his desk to stand beside Carter.

They formed a wall in front of Spence. He would have to get around both of them to get out of there.

"What is this?" Spence looked back and forth between his two brothers. "You can't believe she's working with Jeff."

Derrick scoffed. "Of course not."

"She's not the type," Carter added as he shook his head.

Some of the indignation ran out of Spence then. He thought he was going to have to come to her defense, explain it to them. There was no way she would do what Jeff suggested. She'd had multiple chances to screw them all over and never took one. That's not how she operated. When she was ticked off, she fought the battle head-on. Spence knew because he'd gone more than a few rounds with her.

One of the things he loved about her was her refusal to back down. She fought for what she believed in and refused to be shoved around or forgotten. He found that drive, that will, so sexy.

"Then what's the problem with me going after her?" Spence asked because he really didn't get it.

Carter made a hissing sound. "See, you questioned her."

"No..."

Derrick nodded. "You did."

That didn't happen. "I never believed the note from Jeff."

"I wanted an explanation, which is fine. I'm not sleeping with her. But once she gave it, I was all in on her side." Carter winced. "But you questioned why she didn't let you rescue her."

"Women hate that sort of thing where you rush in and try to save the day without talking to them first." Derrick shrugged. "Or so I've been told by Ellie about a thousand times."

They had both lost it. Spence didn't understand what they didn't get about this situation. "We're dating."

Carter nodded. "Uh-huh."

"I'm in love with her."

Derrick clapped Spence on the back. "There it is."

Carter whistled. "Finally."

It was as if they had the code to some secret language he didn't have. "I hate you both right now."

"You and Abby need to learn how to communicate." Derrick made that pronouncement as he returned to his oversize desk chair and sat down.

"If you're ready to do that, you should go find her. If not…" Carter shook his head. "I'd wait until I had an epiphany."

"I don't know what either of you are talking about." Spence didn't. Advice swam around in his head. Competing feelings of frustration and desperation battled inside him. He didn't want the rift between them to grow. But he wasn't quite sure what he needed to do, either.

Then there was the baby. That issue never left his mind. Bringing the possibility up now to Abby might get him punched. Even he was smart enough to know he needed to keep whatever was brewing between them separate from family talk.

He tried to come up with the right question to ask as Derrick picked up the phone. "Who are you calling?"

"It's time Jeff Berger and I meet."

"Do it in public and don't run him over with a car," Carter said. "If you do, make it look like an accident."

Through the haze of confusion one thought settled in Spence's mind. His brothers really did trust and believe Abby. She told her side and they fell into line.

Maybe now it was his turn.

Forget waiting. Now was the right time. He headed for the door.

Derrick hung up the phone again without dialing. "Where are you going?"

"To find Abby."

"I guess that means you've had that epiphany," Carter said, sounding pretty pleased with himself.

"No, but I'm hoping it will hit me on the way." Spence's fingers touched the door handle before he glanced back at Derrick. "I'll leave Jeff to you. If I confront him right now, I might kill him."

"Consider him handled."

One problem down. Now Spence had the bigger one to conquer.

Fifteen

Abby paced back and forth in her office. It felt as if hours had passed, but she knew that wasn't true. She couldn't see the clock or hear any noise. Her curt order to her assistant to hold all of her calls and visitors—something she'd apologize for later—probabiy said enough for the people outside her door to scurry away.

She wasn't one to close the door and demand peace. When she did, people knew it meant something. Since the gossip about her love life and dating Spence swirled around the office, some might even figure out the source of her frustration.

The chill refused to leave her bones. She had no idea how it was possible to feel hot and ice-cold at the same time, but there she was. The pain in her stomach and her head. Both thumped, demanding attention.

She didn't even hear the door open. She turned, thinking to go in search of something for the headache, and ran right into Spence's broad chest. He reached for her arms and held her, more to keep her from falling than anything else. This wasn't a hug. There was nothing intimate about it. More of a safety-first sort of thing.

He steadied her then reached back to close the door. There, that would stop the gossip. Abby almost rolled hers eyes at the novice move.

"What are you doing here?" She thought for sure he'd hide in Derrick's office all day. If he had a home, he might go there but he didn't. And that bothered her, too.

All of her confusion and questions balled up together. He'd left the last time. There was nothing stopping him from going again. His reaction to the baby had been almost perfect. Sure, he wavered a bit at first but so did she. But she sensed he was waiting to see if this whole visit-home-to-Derrick thing worked out.

His hands dropped to his sides as he looked down at her. "This time you ran."

She searched his face for any sign that they were going to be okay. Not that she wanted a handwritten agreement signed in blood. She didn't even require some sort of long-term commitment, though her heart begged for one. But everything about him, from the fact he lived out of a bag to his office that still looked like no one had been assigned there, showed that he lived his life in a temporary fashion. She didn't know why the Jeff Berger situation drove that point home, but it did.

Now what?

"I needed space," she said, knowing it sounded trite and was only half-correct.

He nodded. "I get it."

That just made the confusion inside her spin faster. "Do you?"

When he frowned at her, she decided to take hold of the conversation. That might be the only way to get through this. Then she could go home and curl up on the couch and forget everything about the last few weeks. Go back to building emotional walls and burying herself in projects in the office.

"Why haven't you started any new projects at work?" It was so simple that she wondered why she hadn't seen it before.

His eyes widened. "What?"

The response was fair. She hadn't exactly built up to it, but the topic was not going away. It had taken hold in her head and she had to ride it out now. "You're the head of new acquisitions. I think that's the fancy title, right? But I haven't seen you do one lick of work on anything but projects already in progress."

His hands went to his hips and a look of pure disbelief crossed his face. He looked ten seconds from exploding. "You're giving me a work evaluation?"

She couldn't tell if he was stalling while his mind

came up with a snappy answer or if he really didn't understand how he came off to the world. "You're great at the job. I doubt you even realize how good you are. It's a natural skill for you. People listen to you. You're organized. You can get things moving and straightened out. You've been the perfect closer."

He shook his head. "What does any of this have to do with Jeff Berger?"

Nothing, everything. She wasn't sure how to explain how it all came together in her head, so she didn't even try.

She moved away from him, slipped behind her desk. Stood with her hands on the back of her chair. It provided a wall of sorts, a shield for what she feared was to come. "This issue is so much bigger than him."

He threw his hands up. "Fill me in because I'm lost."

But that tone. He wasn't engaged and listening, wanting to get it. That tone was defensive. It was the one he used as he prepared for verbal battle. She'd heard it before. He used it on business associates and on her.

It meant he was already closing a door. She could almost feel it slam shut on her.

"You're a good closer because what's required of that job is wrapping up and moving on. Your specialty area." It seemed so clear to her now. No wonder he volunteered to handle those tasks for Derrick while Ellie was on bed rest.

"We're back to talking about my dad and what happened back then?" Spence rested his palms against her desk. Leaned down and faced off with her right over her desk. "Are you kidding me? I thought we moved forward."

"When?"

"Isn't that what the sex was about?"

The walls shook from the force of his voice. She glanced at the door, happy that it was closed. But people walking by had to know a fight waged in her office.

Let them listen.

She struggled to keep her voice calm. Did not let him see that the sex comment slashed through her. "Have we ever dealt with the underlying issue?"

"That you're afraid of commitment."

Her mouth dropped open. She felt it go. "Me?"

He pushed off the desk and stood up straight again. "You are so sure people are going to leave you."

The comment hit its mark. She felt it right to the center of her chest. But he was missing a very important piece of this puzzle. "You did leave me."

"I messed up, Abby. I am sorry." He turned away from her for a second and wiped a hand through his hair. When he looked at her again, his eyes were wild. It was as if the warring inside him was tearing him apart. "I will say it to you however many times it takes to make it better for you. Just tell me."

It was so tempting to drop the subject. Go to him, hug it out. Pretend that this subject and the worry wouldn't haunt her nights...but it would.

"Promise me you won't do it again." It was an impossible request. So unfair of her, and she knew that. She just didn't know how else to say what she needed.

She'd spent a lifetime losing the people she loved. She closed the circle, only let a few in. But the point was she *had* let him in. Now she worried he was clawing against the walls to get out again.

"I...what are you talking about?" His voice came out as a ragged whisper.

"Jeff's stuff was another hole you could slip through. An excuse you could use to go."

Spence shook his head. His voice carried a pleading tone now. "I didn't. I stood in that office and defended you."

"You wanted to know why I didn't tell you about Jeff and his threats." The words stuck in her throat but she pushed them out. She'd only just figured out half of this herself, and it sucked to dump it on him. But it was about him. "In part, I wanted to handle it. Not give Derrick another burden. Back then, not give him a reason to doubt me because he was my boss and you were gone."

"Sure, that makes sense."

"This time, I kept it quiet so *you* wouldn't have a reason to doubt me."

His shoulders fell, as if the will had run right out of him. "You are confusing all of these things. They aren't related to each other."

"I can't wait around for you to leave me again." She almost sobbed when she said it, but there it was. The real fear. The one that spun around inside her, getting bigger, grabbing on to everything. It tainted the good times and made the idea of being pregnant almost impossible to bear.

His eyes looked empty now. The voice, the way he stood there, as if his muscles had stopped working. It all suggested that he was lost. She would do anything to lead him back to her, but he had to help her. He needed to recognize that this was an issue and fight with her.

"How about trusting me enough to know I'm going to stay."

The words pummeled her. "Trust is earned."

"You're saying I don't deserve it." It wasn't a question. He said it as a statement of fact.

That's not how she meant it. She did not see him as a lost cause. He was smart and funny, charming and sexy. He had a bone-deep loyalty, because that is why he came back to help Derrick. Not out of curiosity.

He was her everything and could be all she ever wanted. When she looked at him she knew she'd love him forever.

That realization had her pressing her hand against her chest. "I haven't seen many clues that you intend to put down roots. No house. No new work."

He made a strangled sound. "You and the baby. The *maybe* baby."

All the hope ran out of her then. She leaned harder against the chair to keep from falling to the floor. "That's exactly the wrong answer."

"Why?"

"I need you to stay because you want to, not because you have to." It was just that simple. After a lifetime of settling for limited friendships and not going too deep, she wanted it all. "Until you make a decision about that, you need to stay away."

"Abby." He reached for her.

She was already moving. She held open the door, knowing he would go. He should. The things he needed to decide had to be done without her. All she could do was hope he'd come back. "The choice is yours."

Later that night, after ignoring a series of Jameson-related calls and Jackson's knock at the door, Abby sat on her couch. She'd put on her sweatpants and curled up in the corner. The move usually made her feel better, but not this time.

She wasn't alone, but she didn't blame the company. It was hard to get angry with a pregnant woman who refused to leave the hallway until Abby let her in. Stubbornness ran deep in Ellie.

"Are you supposed to be out of bed?" Abby asked for the third time.

Ellie didn't take the hint. She leaned into the cushions and rubbed her nonexistent belly. "This sounded like an emergency."

Not that Abby had thrown up the white flag. She'd purposely not bothered Ellie because she didn't want to upset her. She also didn't want Ellie getting together with another Jameson and ganging up on Spence. He needed to come to whatever conclusion he came to on his own.

Just thinking about that sent a new wave of sadness crashing through Abby. Spence was the type

who did better with a little guidance. He was someone her grandmother would say *needed a good
woman*. Abby really wanted to be that.

Since she didn't squeal, Abby knew that left a few
suspects. "Derrick told you about what happened in
the office."

Abby was pretty sure her fight with Spence had
already made the rounds at the company. They hadn't
been quiet. And the look on his face as he walked
out of her office. She felt like she'd kicked a puppy.

"Derrick and Carter told Jackson, who called me.
Then Derrick texted. Carter came by the house." Ellie
cited the list in a singsongy voice. "Honestly, it was this
weird chain of communication from Jameson men."

Abby noticed one name was missing. "Not all of
them."

"No, Spence is likely afraid of me right now,
which is not a bad thing."

Ellie's smile was almost chilling. Abby hated to
think what that meant. "What did you do?"

"Told him to stop being a—" Ellie's voice cut off
as she waved a hand in the air. "That's enough about
him. How are you?"

Nice try. "A mess."

Ellie put a pillow in front of her and held on to it
like a life jacket. "I can see that."

"Thanks." She owned a mirror. She knew.

"But the look is familiar. I had it when I thought
Derrick and I were over."

Abby still couldn't believe that happened. "You
two are so obviously perfect for each other."

Ellie snorted. "So, you can see it in others just not in your own life."

They'd circled right back to Spence. No surprise there. Abby was impressed with how quickly Ellie managed it. "You're lucky you're pregnant."

"Spill." Ellie threw the pillow to the side and shifted so that she sat sideways on the couch, facing Abby. "Now. I have a ticking clock here. Jackson brought me over. Once Derrick figures that out, he'll yell this building down."

Rather than debate about where she should be, Abby dove in. What was the harm in reliving this disaster one more time? "You heard about Jeff Berger."

Ellie nodded. "Yep, unfortunately. And if I never hear his name again, I'll be thrilled."

"Same here." Some of the energy ran out of Abby there. She'd been holding it together, but only by a thread. When she looked at Ellie's face now, she wanted to just get the rest out. "He's a runner, Ellie."

Ellie frowned. "This Berger guy?"

"You know who I'm talking about. He hasn't settled in. He's living out of your house and mine. His workload is a mix of odds and ends, other people's stuff." Abby cut off the list before it got so long that it strangled the last little bit of hope inside her. "You know he could pick up again."

"You're jumping around. First, this Berger guy. Now the running thing."

"It's all part of the same problem." At least it was in Abby's head. "He's looking for reasons to go. I tie him here. Other things tie him here. But does he really want to be here? I just feel like he's hiding things."

Ellie made a humming sound. "Like you did when you withheld the details of this Berger guy's threats."

Okay...well...that was an annoying comparison. "It's not the same thing."

"Sure it is. It's all about trust. Neither of you have moved past what happened before and forgiven each other."

Abby got stuck on the "neither" part. "What did I do?"

"Oh, most of the blame goes to Spence and his father. But how much of a fight did you put up?" Ellie's eyebrow lifted. "I'm betting you assumed Spence would leave, because your life is easier when you don't connect with people all that much. Then he confirmed your worst fears. Rather than yelling at him like he deserved, you retreated."

That was ridiculous...wasn't it? "I don't retreat."

Ellie let out an annoying snort. A pretty loud one, too. "Do you love him?"

Abby didn't stall or gloss over the question. She hit it head-on. "More than anything."

It felt weird to say the words. To hear them out there. She did love him. Like, couldn't-think-straight love him.

"Then let him in and insist he do the same with you." Ellie smiled as if she'd solved all the world's problems. "As an objective observer, neither of you is going anywhere."

"I'm not." Abby was hoping he wasn't. Which

meant only one thing. Ellie was right. "You sort of make some sense. Kind of."

"That must have hurt to admit."

Abby made a face. "A little."

"Good." When Abby started to say something, Ellie held up her hand. "I mean it's good because the rest of the family is exhausted by the inability of both of you otherwise very smart people to figure this out."

This was the lecture Abby never expected to hear, but it made her feel better. She'd been blaming him and waiting for him to step up. Maybe she needed to make it clear that she could take a step, too. "Nice delivery."

Ellie's demeanor changed. She grew serious as she reached out and grabbed Abby's hand. "Trust him, Abby. Then maybe leave a little room to trust yourself."

Abby realized that for a person who didn't have many friends, she sure did pick the right ones. "Thanks."

Ellie gave Abby's hand another squeeze before she let go. "Before you do anything, do you think we can convince Jackson to get us some food?"

"It is one of his many skills."

"Good man."

Sixteen

Spence sat on the edge of his bed at Derrick's place, trying to reason out what Abby had said. He still thought she'd mixed up events and created a big thing that didn't exist. The running away issue...he had to own up to that. It was his go-to move and giving it up would take everything he had.

But he'd do it for her. He'd do almost anything for her.

"Why are you here?"

Spence looked up to find Derrick leaning in the doorway. He looked comfortable. Like a man who had finally found some peace At least until the screaming baby came.

"That's welcoming." Spence didn't bother to get up or move over. He knew Derrick would loom there, waiting for the right time to impart some wisdom. That was *his* go-to move.

Derrick let out a long and very loud exhale. "You should be at Abby's, insisting you two can work things out."

"Can we?" That was the question that kept bouncing around in Spence's head. He'd never wanted anything this much.

"You know the answer. You're just feeling sorry for yourself."

As pep talks went, this was not one of Derrick's better ones. Spence was hoping for more. "Thanks, man."

"You have a right to. Your life is a mess." Derrick did step inside then. He walked over and sat next to Spence. "But she's the right one for you and you know that. Put away the fear and set down roots. You belong here. You belong with her."

He sounded like Abby. Their comments mirrored each other. Apparently, everyone else could see his fear. So much for the theory he did a good job of hiding it. "You make it sound easy."

Derrick laughed. "Oh, it's scary as hell. I know."

"And I have this." Spence reached beside him and picked up the unopened envelope from Eldrick. This was part of the requirements that would allow Derrick to take over the business. What needed to be done to make Eldrick slip away permanently, because Spence knew Derrick feared Dad would just walk into the office one day and try to run things again. The ownership percentages allowed him to do it.

"Open it." Derrick shrugged, acting as if his entire business future didn't ride on whatever was inside. "You may as well face everything at once. Let's see if you balk."

Spence ripped the top open. "And my list of requirements is…wait."

The air punched out of his lungs. Spence blinked a few times, trying to bring the simple sentences into focus. This wasn't a legal document; it was… he didn't know what it was.

Derrick frowned as he grabbed the paper out of Spence's hands. "What?"

Go find Abigail. Beg her to take you back. She never betrayed you.

"Come on. Is our dad taking responsibility for something? That can't be right." It seemed impossible. Spence couldn't even get the words to register in his brain.

"Yes, but even weirder, I think he's matchmaking." Derrick turned the paper over then flipped it back again. "This can't be from Beth or her doing. The envelope was here long before the engagement party, and that's where she found out. That's all Dad."

"Our dad?" The one who harassed Abby and kissed her. The one who sent them down this awful road. "No way."

"Apparently people can change." Derrick handed the paper back to Spence. "Your turn."

* * *

An hour later, Spence stood at Abby's door. Without saying a word, she gestured for him to step inside. Didn't slam the door on his face.

That alone seemed like a step forward. "Thanks for letting me come in."

"You still have the key and the security codes."

Some of the hope inside him died. Her voice sounded flat and there was nothing welcoming about a conversation about security codes. "Is that why you agreed to see me?"

She stopped in the middle of her living room and faced him. She wore oversize sweatpants and a T-shirt with a rip along the shoulder seam. Her hair was half in and half out of a ponytail holder.

She had never looked more beautiful to him.

She sighed. "No, I agreed because I love you."

His mind went blank and his mouth went dry. He was pretty sure he made that up in his head. There was no way she said those words. "What?"

"There, I said it. I love you." She threw up her hands then let them drop to her sides again. "You ran out on me, and I am terrified you will do it again, but that's the truth. I love you, you big moron."

He was even fine with the last part. "Abby—"

"I believe in you even though you don't believe in yourself."

His brain finally signaled his legs to move. In a few steps, he was in front of her, had his hands on her waist and pulled her in closer to him. "Don't stop."

She frowned at him. "What?"

They *really* did need to work on their communication skills. He decided to start now. "I can't deny that there's this whirling sensation inside me. When things blow up and a fight that could shred everything looms, I go. It stops the arguing and I can catch my breath. I've been using that defense mechanism since I was a kid."

She started to pull away. "Right."

"Not with you." He hugged her even tighter. Pressed his lips against her eyebrow in a kiss that was meant mostly to soothe her but ended up calming him. When he pulled back, some of the wariness had left her eyes. "See, every other time, I walked away and the feelings, the churning, the reason I fled in the first place, disappeared. With you, the need only got stronger."

Her fingers clenched against his forearms. "You didn't come back to me. I waited for some sign. Any sign."

"I felt broken, Abby. I knew I had already fallen for you and then my dad…" Mentioning him could ruin everything. He wasn't the problem between them now. Not really. "Forget that. This was my fault. I left and I missed you every single day. I couldn't visit my brother because I worried I would see you."

She nibbled on her bottom lip. For a few seconds, she didn't say anything and he held his breath…waiting.

When nothing happened, he tried again. "It was a crappy thing to leave and then to make you wait. You suffered. I suffered. I don't want to do it anymore."

She brushed her fingertip over his bottom lip. "Can you break the cycle?"

She'd asked the question but he sensed she was starting to believe. To hope.

"Before you told me about the possible pregnancy, I wanted to tell you how I felt." He nodded toward the living room. "Sitting right there on that couch, I was going to tell you I loved you. That I'd figured out I would always love you. That you were worth sticking around and fighting through the mess."

Tears gathered in her eyes. "Spence."

He rushed to get the rest out. "I didn't tell you then because I didn't want you to think I did it because I had to, but I'll tell you now." He rested his forehead against hers and inhaled. "Baby or not, I want to build a life with you. That gnawing sense of wanting to bolt will likely always be with me, but I don't want to leave you. Ever."

She wrapped her arms around his neck. "Sounds like I'd have to go with you then."

The words were muffled in his neck, but he heard them. Also picked up on the happiness in her tone. How much lighter she sounded.

"That also works." He lifted her head and stared down into her eyes. "But really, I love my brothers. I've even gotten used to the office, which is nothing short of a miracle."

She smiled. "What are you saying?"

He recognized hope when he saw it. It soared through him, too. "Take a chance on me. I know I'm a risk, but—"

"Stop." She shrugged as she hugged him close. "It's too late. My life is already bound up with yours. I'm afraid you're stuck with me."

"I love the sound of that." He kissed her. Let his lips linger over hers, loving the feel of her body pressed against his.

"Good, because I plan on making it a requirement for the next fifty years or so."

He didn't try to fight the smile. "Then we should start now."

"I like your style."

It was well past two in the morning. They were in bed, lying side by side, recovering from what she might call the greatest make-up sex of all time. She'd mentioned that to him and he hadn't stopped smiling. Until right now.

She looked at his hands, those long fingers. Saw the white stick he held in a death grip. "You keep staring at it."

"It's so little and has the power to change everything with a plus sign."

He'd insisted on the pregnancy test after their last round. She'd wanted cake, but he won the argument. Now, if only the panic screaming through her would stop.

"I could make a joke about how babies disrupt lives, but I'm not sure you're ready for that." She also wanted to point out that the Jameson men were pretty fertile and warn Carter, but the timing seemed wrong for that, too.

Spence shook the stick. "It should do something."

"Like?"

He shrugged. "Balloons should pop out of it. Maybe play music."

"It's not a magic stick."

He snorted as his head turned and he faced her. "It kind of is. We wave it and it changes everything about our lives together."

Skipping the cake might have been smart. Her stomach wouldn't stop dancing. "Well, that's true."

His eyes narrowed just a fraction. "You okay?"

"Scared." It would take her a while to figure out how to deal with this news. They'd have to make plans, but she knew they would do it together. He'd made that clear. "Not about us. Not about how much I love you."

He turned over and faced her. Wrapped an arm around her waist as he watched her. "But?"

"This is going to be hard. We're still trying to sort ourselves out as a couple and now we'll have this." A few hours ago, that would have terrified her, but not as much now. She just needed to make sure he agreed with her. "Spence, this is—"

"I'm going to get angry if you offer me an out."

"Six weeks ago, when you stepped back into my life, I knew you as the guy who bolted when everything got to be too much." She winced as she pointed that out. She didn't want to start another fight.

"Didn't we settle this?" But he didn't sound angry. Instead, he rolled her onto her back and balanced his body over hers.

She ran a hand up and down his bare arm, loving the feel of his sleek muscles under her fingertips. "I trust you to stay. The point is I want you to."

"Leaving you, losing you, ripped me apart." He pressed a quick kiss on the tip of her nose. "It was a wake-up call for me to get my act together."

She let the words settle in her head. Yeah, she liked the sound of that. A lot. "And I'm part of that act?"

He snorted. "You have the main role in it."

The last of her defenses crumbled. The walls came roaring down and took her doubts with them. In a few short hours, with a couple of words, he brought her peace. It would not be easy. Knowing the two of them, life would not be quiet or simple. It would be loud and loving and perfectly imperfect, and that sounded pretty great to her.

"I love you. You and your big messy family." Because when she claimed him, she decided she'd claim them, too. "Okay, not your dad."

"Remind me to show you something later." His smile was downright mysterious. "A letter."

She didn't want to know, yet part of her did. She guessed he did that on purpose. Reeled her in and made her care about Eldrick, which should have been an impossible feat.

"I hate letters right now." They reminded her of Jeff and no matter how tonight turned out, she still despised that guy.

Spence's smile only grew wider. "This one may surprise you."

"I'm intrigued." She was about to pepper him

with questions, but his hand slipped under the covers. Right down to her thigh. "Oh, yeah. There." Then those expert fingers traveled a big higher. "The letter can wait."

"Yes, it can."

"I'm going to let you show me how much you love me."

He rolled over her then. "Again?"

"I'm sure you can handle it."

He lowered his mouth until it hovered right above hers. "I can handle you."

"Show me."

* * * * *

Don't miss the first JAMESON HEIRS *novel*

PREGNANT BY THE CEO
by HelenKay Dimon

Available now from Harlequin Desire!

***

If you're on Twitter, tell us what you think of
Harlequin Desire! #harlequindesire